MIRRORSTRIKE

BENJANUN SRIDUANGKAEW

Cover art by Anna Dittman.

Jacket design by Mikio Murikami.

ISBN TPB 978-1-937009-73-1

Also available as a DRM-free eBook.

Apex Publications, PO Box 24323, Lexington, KY 40524

Visit us at www.apexbookcompany.com.

TWO TO BIND

IN THE HOUSE of the Winter Queen, even time itself slows.

Above Nuawa, the prisoner swings in shallow parabolas, a human pendulum suspended by iron and harness. She has never thought a body could be reduced so small. Ytoba is little more than a torso, ice clinging to the stumps where eir limbs used to be. By right ey should have long succumbed. She was the one to hack those limbs off and she was not delicate about the task—the hemorrhage alone should have been fatal. Somehow ey persists.

At the moment, Ytoba is wearing the face of Nuawa's mother, Indrahi.

As Nuawa understands it, the act of shifting shapes costs em: like any other physical exertion it places demands on the flesh. Ey hasn't been fed much recently, only water and the thinnest gruel, the occasional rice boiled to soft mush. She is sure—she has personally been forcing every watery spoonful down eir throat. It should have left em too malnourished to think, let alone alter eir shape, to her mother's or anyone else's.

"Are you," ey whispers with her mother's voice, "going to kill me again?"

"I'm aware of who and what you are, and my mother's ghost you are not." She gazes at the frieze behind em, gray ice and blue glass on the wall, water crystals arranged into the shape of hyacinths, Her Majesty's flower. Here even the prison cells are beautiful, the same way moraines are. "There's no real point in keeping you, save for the general's sentiment. She may show you mercy. I have no interest."

Ey smiles. Her mother's mouth. "Afraid I might betray you by revealing what you were up to? Exposing you to the prince. Though I'm sure you'll never let me have audience with her."

Nuawa shows em her wrist, where the hyacinth glints like a small faceted knife. "I've been sworn in, and General Lussadh has even less interest in speaking to you than I do." The general being half a continent away.

"There are laws and forces you're dealing with that you fail to understand. One to wake. Two to bind. By and by you shall lose your will, become the queen's creature in truth as well as pretense. Your mother's plot and her legacy wearing thin, then wearing out, then simply wiped away. I am sure your mother will be proud." Ey gazes at her unblinking. "And you're dying too, aren't you?"

"Am I? Every minute we're dying. Some faster than others."

"I'm an expert. I can smell poison—some parasite. Very creative. It's not contagious though, not until it spawns, and by that point you'd be in no state to spread it anywhere. If you mean to assassinate Prince Lussadh during intimacy, this is an exceptionally poor method."

Impotent taunts, until the end. "This is all you have to say?"

"What did you reckon? That I would give you the queen's secrets? After you've done so much for me." The smile widens and, at last, it no longer resembles her mother's: toothed, grotesquely wide. Further than any human mouth should be able to stretch. "Anything I know will have to go with me to the next earth."

"Well," she says, drawing her gun, "that is that, then."

The ice shudders to gunfire acoustics, a few icicles falling off, tinkling a pretty, abortive melody. The assassin sags in the harness. In death ey does not revert to eir true face, true shape. In death, ey looks almost like Indrahi when Nuawa shot her.

But she is no child, and can separate fact from fantasy. She loosens the harness, turns the torso around, checking for a pulse one last time. There is none. For good measure, she slits the shapeshifter's throat.

Even in this chill, the arterial system still has power; the blood leaves em in a burst, drenching her sleeves. The rest puddles under em, soaking the harness and the frost tiles. More black than red, under this light.

"This is for you, Mother," she says, but there is no answer. Only the cold, the dark, and the weight of history like a noose around her throat.

ONE

LUSSADH HUNTS. The night is deep and the frosted roofs gleaming with ice, but she is used to both. She moves with precision, a foot in a crack between slates, another on a ledge that would bear her weight but only just. It is quiet. Cities under siege always are: she knows from experience, having been on both the defending and invading ends. For those defending, familiar streets and intersections distort; all laws and rules shift to accommodate the factors of combat always impending.

She glances briefly behind her shoulder, in the direction where her army camps, awaiting her next command. From this distance they are not visible, obscured by the high, high walls. Citizens of Kemiraj may even pretend they are at peace and that their magistrate has not revolted against the Winter Queen. She turns her gaze back to her destination, inhaling the clean, crystalline air. When was it that she's become at home wherever snow is, has taken the queen's element as her own? It must have been gradual, but it has happened so seamlessly that she no longer remembers a time when she felt otherwise and called herself a child of the desert.

Not that there's much desert left, now.

A step, then another. She climbs until there is no further handhold and no further roof. A gap yawns between the platform she occupies and the top of the wall that protects the magistrate's mansion. She judges the distance, draws back, and leaps.

She lands easily, with minimal noise. A matter of training—from her youth she was tutored by court assassins—and a matter of agility granted by the queen's mirror. The slight, subtle strengths that together come to something more. Lussadh will be fifty soon and hardly feels the fact. Her body may not be the tireless engine it was at sixteen or twenty-five, but it remains formidable, lightly touched by age. Joints and muscles well-oiled as ever. A day will come when all these fail, but through her queen's blessing, that is yet held at bay.

Through the garden she moves, concealed by shadow and a veil of aversion made by one of her officers. Not the most potent thaumaturgy, but it deflects attention, makes her peripheral to the naked sight. Major Guryin is practiced at such things, the minor alterations, the tricks of perception. It would not hold against direct scrutiny. Still she has little enough to worry about. The city's military falls into two categories: loyal to winter and therefore dead—Magistrate Sareha executed them with the suddenness of garrotes in the dark—or loyal to Sareha and therefore vanishingly few. Of that handful, most have been decimated by Lussadh's army. Sareha would not be able to muster more than ten soldiers to defend her estate.

The grass is nearly as tall as she is, the trees black and dense.

She feels more than hears the velocity of it, the metal cutting through the air. Time enough to turn so the shard buries itself in her right shoulder instead of her throat. She drops to her knees, half-hidden in the shrubs, her back against the base of a marble plinth. Smaller target this way. Her breathing judders.

Lussadh doesn't try to extract the flechette. It has gone in too deep, piercing armor as though it is paper instead of reinforced mesh, and the tip is not tidy. Someone knew she would be here, and that she'd wear armor witched to blunt the brute force of a bullet. Needle guns are uncommon, an occidental invention and a specialist's choice. Short range. She searches overhead, in the rough direction the shot originated. Nothing. Like her, the sniper must have upon them a charm that averts sight. But now she knows what to look for and, as tempting a target as she is, the next shot must come.

A glint, handgrip or barrel. Even painted for nocturnal use, a needle gun is mostly metal.

She switches hands, takes aim, fires. Her tutors impressed upon her the importance of being able to shoot with either hand.

The would-be assassin falls like an overripe fruit. Lussadh touches her calling-glass and says, "Guryin. Fly your scout low."

Instantly the hawk-shadow that has been trailing her plunges into the canopies, a thing of etheric wings like knives. Entirely silent. Another body drops. The hawk-shadow emerges again and propels forward, the momentum of a bullet.

"You're clear, General." The major's pause is slight but admonitive. "Are you going ahead?"

"It seems wasteful not to."

A truncated sigh. "The magistrate is on the second floor. Up the stairs, turn left, end of corridor. There's no other security that I can detect, thaumaturgic or otherwise—this time I've made sure. My apologies for that one stray."

Guryin does not inquire as to the state of her wound, trusting that Lussadh can make her own judgment. Which she can, though perhaps the major is not wrong that going forward here is unwise. She stands: the pain has receded a little, the way sensation numbs in extreme cold, and the bleeding has slowed to a trickle. Left untreated it can still kill, but for now she can push on.

True to Guryin's word, no other surprise awaits her on the manor ground or inside the building itself. Fortunate that the magistrate has retreated to her mansion rather than occupy the al-Kattan palace. No doubt both because the manor is easier to defend—smaller area, fewer points of exit and entry—but also because the palace would not abide Magistrate Sareha's treachery. The living architecture, after all this time, still answers to al-Kattan blood first and foremost. The moment news of the uprising reached Lussadh, she'd willed its gates and doors to clench shut. But by then Sareha had fled the palace, holing herself up in her own manor.

The house is well-lit. Lussadh passes long dining tables that have been set for ten, for dozens. Beautiful enameled plates rimmed with bird-faced dancers, brass spoons and samovars, and thread of gold in the tablecloth. She goes up the stairs. It is a short corridor, and the door in question is unlocked.

Magistrate Sareha sits by the window. She is stooped, a woman who was not young when Lussadh selected her from a clerical post in Shuriam; she closes in on eighty now. Without looking at Lussadh, she says, "You should be in too much pain to move, and bleeding buckets besides. It's true what they say, that you've become a demon after you submitted to the queen."

Suspension or postponement of time is not the same as immortality, but Lussadh does not quibble the difference. There is use in being thought of as preternatural. "I've come to offer you mercy."

The old woman does not laugh. Instead she stands and draws a machete. The blade is curved inward, graceful. "I'm old and weak. You're injured, though unnatural. Fight me. It will not be fair, but it will give me dignity."

"I fear I must decline." The appeal upon her chivalry, which Lussadh supposes she is famous for. She does understand her magistrate's pride: the last stand, the final gesture. But she has no intention of indulging it, and her wounded shoulder is throbbing like a heart about to go into cardiac arrest. "These are your choices: Surrender and answer my questions, and I'll give you death without the kiln. Refuse and I will disable you, and give your soul to the queen's service, as is right for high treason."

Now Sareha does laugh. "As I understand, the ghosts aren't really sentient. Mindless shadows are all they are, and all I will be in that state. Mercy you call it, when dignified death should be everyone's by right. Even the most bloodthirsty tyrants of Kemiraj left our souls alone. But either way, I won't be around to care."

"I swore you in and assigned you this post, to govern Kemiraj when my aide and I are away. I lifted you up from the bones and mud of Shuriam. Why this?"

"I've been dying for years—an illness of the blood, you see, and age. There's nothing left for me to lose and I have hated your queen for decades. I've hated the al-Kattan for longer still, for who was it that reduced my home Shuriam to mud and our beautiful fastnesses to ruin?" The old woman hefts the machete, turning it this way and that, the blade catching light. "There comes a point when you must make a decision, and I wanted to show you that even a dying old woman may upset your order, even just for a month or two, and massacre more than two hundred pledged to your army."

The tally is closer to three hundred, most of them infantry and recruits native to Kemiraj. It was swift and comprehensive. Lussadh has to give her that. "I did not invade Shuriam because I wished to," she says. It sounds weak even to her ears.

"But because your grandaunt King Ihsayn ordered it? What a luxury it is, to undertake conquest even though you do not *wish*. If only we could have turned the conquering horde away by virtue of *wishing*." Sareha's voice lilts high, mocking. "It wasn't atonement, Prince Lussadh, when you butchered your own family—that was for your own ambition. It wasn't atonement when you so graciously elevated me—that was for your own guilt, and because you'd executed nearly every Kemiraj official who served Ihsayn. Someone needed to work for you, and I did well, didn't I? How I proved myself and acted the grateful servant who owed you everything."

The old woman lunges. She is right that the days of her strength are ancient history. Lussadh stays out of the magistrate's reach without effort. She lets Sareha swing away, wild and weak, striking at nothing. It is graceless. She takes aim; she shoots to kill. The bullet goes through skull without resistance, so brittle it is, so aged the bone. The body is so light it barely makes sound on the carpet.

Sareha was seventy-five, and there is dignity in dying that old with a weapon in hand, Lussadh thinks. It is what she tells her soldiers in times of low morale.

She holsters her gun and goes to the window where the magistrate was sitting. On the sill there is a handful of ash, gray and fine. Burnt paper, she judges. She gathers the remains into a little cedarwood box lying open close by: a thaumaturge might be able to reconstitute the ash.

Tentatively she parts the curtain. The room is so well lit that all she sees is her own reflection, as Sareha must have before she drew down the drapes. When she was a child, Lussadh thought murder would alter someone so fundamentally that even the appearance must change to match: a shadow that runs a little longer, a countenance darkened by bloody event. By ten or so, she learned that such deeds change very little, inside or outside.

A glint catches her eye, a noise of ice crackling. It is distinct: she is intimately familiar with the harmonics of cold. Just outside the window, a scrim of frost is falling apart. There is shape to it, thin and tall and humanoid. But that quickly dissolves, and soon nothing remains on the pane.

———

IN THE SAFETY of her camp, Lussadh lies back in a divan, groggy from anesthetics. Her wound has been dressed, the flechette removed, and the retaking of Kemiraj is apace. She cannot yet rest and there will be a great deal of labor in days to come. Executing the old woman was more a formality than anything, mostly for Lussadh's sense of closure. The thing that might get her killed, one day, a point that Major Guryin has taken pains to drive home.

A knock on her door. Her aide Ulamat. "My lord," he says, wincing at the sight of her injury. "This was very ill-advised."

"Had we stormed her manor, she'd have committed suicide long before we got there. I wanted to speak to her." She shrugs her furs off —it is warm enough in here, ghost-heated, and she is less susceptible to cold than most. "The why of her coup mattered. It always matters."

"As my lord wishes. But—"

"Yes," Lussadh says.

"You were expected, my lord. There were three people to whom you told your intent to personally venture behind the enemy line. Myself, Major Guryin, and Lieutenant Nuawa."

"I know who I've spoken to. Sareha has known me a long time and could anticipate me perfectly well."

"My lord," Ulamat says, "nevertheless should the queen not be ...?"

She gives him a look. He turns quiet. But she shakes herself and sighs. His concern is not misplaced, and Nuawa's newness is not his fault. And it is not an irrational conclusion to reach. "The queen will not address this the way you or I might. I'll handle it. Has Guryin rounded Sareha's soldiers up?"

"Xe's hunting down stragglers. Xer scouts have located a few, some in groups, some alone. Magistrate Sareha knew what was coming and had ordered those loyal to her to flee. Whoever remains in the city will no doubt claim they were but pretending."

Lussadh grimaces. Presses her knuckles against the skin near her wound, careful not to scratch. "Let Guryin know I want a few prisoners kept for interrogation. Some will volunteer a few names rather than go into the kilns. Cross-examining them should help us sort the true from the false." Though under duress those are not always the right names, and ultimately whatever an officer claims, treason is treason. To actively participate or be quietly complicit amounts to much the same. With an uprising it pays to eliminate loose ends, great or small. Sareha had friends, connections that ran through administrative and military branches like hidden rot. The body that is an empire is as vulnerable as any flesh, perhaps even more, manifold more moving parts, manifold more organs held in secret.

Fatigue catches up with her suddenly—she has been on her feet for eighteen hours. Sieges are grueling things, especially when one cannot simply demolish the gates and break down the walls. Court inventors boast that soon they'll make flying crafts capable of not just ferrying soldiers but to make precision strikes from the air. They boast that war will become as efficient and bloodless as an elegant meal, that the reign of winter will be as impregnable as glaciers and spread across the world entire. Lussadh has tried to imagine this, not the expansion of empire but the aerial strikes, and she cannot. She is no dreamer. She sees what is before her, and prioritizes that.

Then there will be the matter of civilians, what is to be done with them, how their guilt might be determined. Her own subjects. Many will go into the ghost-kilns, young or old, lame or abled, there will be no discriminating. Such a thing has been done before many times, though the queen will be the one who hands out the sentence, absolving Lussadh of the fact. *I shall not allow you to be burdened with guilt,* the queen has told her. *Let me shoulder it. Guilt on you is as rust upon steel.*

Always a weapon. But she has chosen her wielder, and that too matters. Wielding, the heart and constant of all relations, whatever else glazes it, whatever the veneer.

"Go to Guryin," she tells her aide. "I will send a message to the queen."

Ulamat bows and retreats, though not before he fusses over the pot of ginger tea the camp chiurgeon has left for Lussadh. More for his sake than her own she pours a cup and drains it. Aromatic and golden, the way good ginger ought to be. A campaign, even one like this, is no place for luxuries. Nevertheless, Ulamat insists, and her pavilion is absurd in its proportions. The bright flooring, the unnecessary mahogany furniture, the freight carriage for all this. As soon as tomorrow she will reclaim the palace. Already she has plans: soft gloves first, for those can draw out answers, sometimes better than pliers and heated brands.

She covers herself so that the injury will not show, and exhales on her calling-glass.

Nuawa's face appears. On her end she is outdoors, leaning on bleached mothstone, her hair tousled as though she's been walking downwind. "General. I have been waiting to hear from you."

"Much is concluded here." Moving so that the blanket bares half her chest but not the wound, she casually adds, "Perhaps you'd care to join me? I may have to remain here a while, and what a dull time it would be, deprived of your company."

The faintest smile. Nuawa's face is not a mobile one, and her expression is meticulous the way portraits are, precise ink and minimalist color. But sometimes Lussadh catches it lighting up, illuminating from within as though by soft radiance. "We've been apart for less than two months. You cannot already miss me."

"May I not?" She moves a little more, angles herself so that lamplight and shadow sculpt her features. "To wake up beside you each morning. That's what I miss, my newest lieutenant."

Nuawa startles—the surprise is sharp, genuine—and lowers her eyes. Not quite blushing, but flustered. "You don't need to persuade me. You can simply order me there."

"That would be odious of me. Will you come?"

"Yes. Of course."

"Excellent. I'll introduce you formally to one of the other glass-bearers. You still haven't met any of them. Be soon," Lussadh adds softly, "for I'd like to have you in my arms again."

TWO

FOUR MONTHS new to the queen's service as she is, Nuawa has not yet been given anything resembling a duty. Instead she has been left to idle in the capital, and has spent her weeks exploring the palace, its brittle corridors that seem to have been carved from solid glaciers, its immense and often empty halls. Unfurnished for the most part, but sometimes she would open a door—they are unlocked—and she'd find standing all by itself an unused mirror frame. Ornate or plain, made of brass or copper or granite, no two alike. The sight unnerves her more than she would like to admit. She's examined them closely and never found them to be anything but the most ordinary of furniture, and yet there is the inescapable sense that the empty frames are waiting like open mouths.

She climbs to the highest floor, past flights of steep treacherous steps, and emerges on the palace's roof. Her exhalation curls out in white tendrils. From here she can see most of the capital, insofar as it can be called one. More than a city, it is a fastness, chiseled into the shoulder of a mountain and concealed by a long, curved hand of stone and stalagmites. The only real building is the palace itself, the rest lesser edifices raised to accommodate the most ambitious politicians who believe proximity to the throne is synonymous with power. A small hospital, warehouses, and a compound of public bath and teahouse. The nearest train station is far down, two days' trek or—a privilege reserved for the queen's personnel—a vertiginous airdrift.

The air is bitterly frigid; she imagines that to those without a sliver of glass in their hearts, it is like trying to breathe knives. Even insulated in so much fur and sealskin, Nuawa is not impervious. Icicles have gathered on the seams of her hood. But it is a calm day.

Down the sheer roof of a palace wing, two snow-girls are sprinting. They are child-sized but share the features of their larger counterparts, no younger or rounder, no hints that they were ever toddlers or infants. They are giggling soundlessly, hair flaring behind them like stunted wings. They don't wear the hyacinth, but it is not as though what they are—who owns them—can ever be ambiguous. She studies them for a time, tries to picture just what it is that their minds contain, if anything. Theirs is not the remoteness of wolves or hawks. The snow-girls are more like marionettes. Serving no purpose at all, and without instincts of their own. She has never heard them talk and hasn't been able to discover whether they feel pain.

A hand falls on her shoulder and brushes against her cheek. The texture of velvet-sheathed wood, or perhaps cutin. The snow-maid regards her, beaming placidly, and indicates that she should follow. Unlike the others this one is of adult proportions, though still far slighter than Nuawa.

It would be the first audience she has with the queen since her arrival. Since Sirapirat.

The further she ventures into the palace, the less it resembles that which is built for human habitation. The pretense of architecture gives way to craggy outcrops and stalactites, corridor to tunnel, and civilization to cavern. The walls curve, the ice on them like wounds newly scabbed over, blue-black at the core. Nuawa pulls her coat tighter. She licks the inside of her mouth gingerly; for now, her teeth are still bone and enamel rather than rime.

A door gapes at her. An isosceles triangle twice Nuawa's height, built of black steel fringed in turquoise that might be ice or stone. Ghost-lights, in their raw heatless form, illuminate the chamber. The queen has her back to Nuawa, studying a tall object covered in rime-stiffened cloth and snakeskin patchwork. Albino python, black cobra, peridot asp. "My thanks for being prompt, Lieutenant," the queen says. "Go ahead, uncover it. This is for you to see."

The cover does not come free easily, soldered in place by the arctic temperature that radiates from the queen herself. But the moment Nuawa catches a glimpse of the bronze sheen, the half-and-half visage, she lets the cover drop. There is no need to see the rest.

"The assassin told me of what ey offered you and that gave me an ... idea. I'm almost upset that I allowed you to execute em." The queen blends into the room, chameleon, clad in what may well be a dress of rime and tundra. Only her face stands distinct, the eyes like pits. "Modifications will need to be made, but the core and the shell are present."

"Your Majesty, I don't see what you mean."

The queen circles her—she resists the impulse to spin around like a baited dog—and takes her hand from behind. One fingernail, sharp, drags along the creases in her palm, the tributaries. "What do you want, Nuawa? I can grant you so much. Even my general you can have all to yourself, if you badly wish."

Her stomach twitches. "I don't imagine the general would care to be granted to anyone. Save to you."

An exhalation on the nape of her neck, razor-cold. "You underestimate yourself. In all the years she's been in my service she has given her attentions on the most passing of basis. But it is good. I cherish harmony among my best. What monarch or commander could ask for more? And I've been considering assigning you to oversee the governance of Sirapirat. Not immediately, not so soon. To others that may look unseemly, and they'll resent you terribly, wouldn't they? But in a year or two when you're more senior."

To be given what Lussadh has, in every sense, high rank and administration of her home city. Agree, and in submission, be owned. "Your largesse takes my breath away, Your Majesty. What, may I ask, have I done to merit it?"

"Lussadh has summoned you to her country. That is fortuitous, for in Kemiraj lives a mathematician and inventor from whom your assassin nemesis learned much. I'd like you to find this person, and persuade them to work on the god-engine Vahatma for me." The queen lets go. She peels away a fold of snakeskin, sliding it off with languor that veers close to obscene, as though she is undressing the god. "You may tell this inventor whatever lies you like, offer them any reward—true or imaginary. Anything that'll convince them. Their name is Penjarej Manachakul, lately of the Sirapirat Academy of Innovation and Applied Theory."

"And the general?"

"Will be informed of the same task, but you're best suited to this. You do not require her assistance to accomplish so small a duty." A slight tip of the head; the queen's smile is thin-lipped and knowing. "Lussadh says you are a creature of utmost economy. I'm sure you will carry this out flawlessly."

———

ALL TRAINS BOUND for Kemiraj have been rerouted or suspended, save those delivering supplies or personnel to General Lussadh. Belonging to the latter category, Nuawa is given priority. Express train, stopping nowhere, and very fast. She has barely slept before she is woken up by the smells of incense burning. Tidying herself, she leaves her compartment, following the drumbeats and thin smoke.

In the first carriage, the train's priest is refueling the ghosts. A gold-leafed spread of rice, crystallized plantains and pineapples, chocolates and egg-yolk sweets. Five cups of liquor, in black and red and green, and two paper dolls sitting between. "We'll be there in a few hours, Lieutenant," the priest says without looking up from his hand drum or from the lambent cloud of feasting ghosts.

Nuawa peers at the ghosts, trying to discern features, something that'd give an idea that these things were once human. She can't find any, can't even tell how many souls precisely are in that translucent fog. They make indistinct sounds and the gold leaves disappear when they've passed through the food, but in this state they are more like small, tame animals than the dead. Without the offerings and the rites to direct them—animate this train, heat this hospital, push the assembly line in this factory—they would wither and fade, but once they've received their initial instruction, they will keep to them with the steadiness of clocks. "This must be thankless work."

"On the contrary, I am well compensated by the queen." He does not dress like the monks of Sirapirat; rather than saffron he wears white and rather than a bare shaved scalp he keeps his hair underneath a tall, black headpiece. A priest in the Yatpun tradition, devoted to Kidashoten, the one god the queen is known to give prayer. "I prefer to conduct this without company. If you would be so kind."

She considers staying regardless—a court priest is beneath a glass-bearer—and asking him whether he genuinely believes in that foreign and unseen god Kidashoten, or if the queen herself forms the pillar of his faith. Whether she is the one to whom he dedicates his rites. But she returns to her compartment.

She dozes, though never deeply enough for dreams; wakes in time to see Kemiraj's approach. The most beautiful city in winter, it is said, best favored of all territories: a jewel ascendant. She has never before seen it except in broadcasts, in paintings.

The walls first, the color of magnolias, so high that they blot out the sky. The train slows down through a tunnel behind the Gate of Glaives—a checkpoint, one of Kemiraj's defenses—and then upward, climbing a steep incline. A few minutes in the dark and then they are through, on an overpass that leads to the station. Below her the city spreads out, nested gates and garlanded terraces, dome roofs sheathed in brass and copper, and minarets like spears. Stone gardens run along the boundaries that divide districts, ophidian lines that are at points porous, at others solid as steel. From here she cannot see the bottom: Kemiraj is a city that has built upon itself, vertical, looking skyward. Once it was as tall as two storeys, three at the most. Now it is as high as a building of five or seven floors, the tiers overlapping and knotted together, interwoven by immaculate streets.

From this distance, Nuawa cannot spot a single worn façade, a single cracked roof or window. All of Kemiraj is as lustrous as a necklace of pearls, as polished.

The horns blare arrival. She pulls down her luggage—she travels light and leaves most of her belongings in the queen's palace, except for one object. She opens her suitcase to make sure it is there and secure. The diptych is not easy to carry, but there are plenty of hinges and it folds compact. It still takes up most of the suitcase, and she's needed a second case to put her clothes.

She carries them out, two pieces of luggage, for the moment the sum of her life. Nuawa is nearly the only person disembarking, other than a handful of priests and chiurgeons. Most of the train's freight is supplies.

"Let me take that for you."

"To think I'd have winter's commander as my porter." She lets Lussadh handle the heavier suitcase—the diptych will be seen eventually, and she means to be casual about it. No point rousing suspicion when it is only a sentimental object. "You spoil me, General."

Lussadh leads her to the near-empty depot. There are traces of traffic and commerce—stains of food and mud on the ground—but they are hollow records. The only human presence is military. But even in this condition the station is prettily made, ziggurat chandeliers golden with ghosts, the wall mosaics kept fresh with witching or repainting. "Is that not my prerogative, to spoil whomever I wish?" the general is saying. "How was your journey?"

There is no limp or weakness to the way Lussadh moves, but the general is delicate with her right side. A bicep injury, Nuawa judges, and not the harmless and incidental sort like a pulled ligament. It is a wound, as yet tender. "Comfortable. But not half as luxurious as it is to be in your presence."

"You're a brazen flatterer. Have you been here before?"

"No, I've never had cause." To look on this concentration of winter's favor and funds, and to remember how much has been stripped from Sirapirat, ghost-tax and otherwise. "It's warmer than I expected." Still not warm, still hardly summer, but where the rest of the territories are frigid, here the cold is tolerable. The citizens of Kemiraj require much less ghost-heat than elsewhere, need to spend much less on warm clothing.

Lussadh's expression flickers. "Much colder than it once was."

It is the first time she has witnessed something like ambiguity when it comes to the general's opinion on what the queen has done to her territories, the altering and erasing of topography. Nuawa makes herself smile. "The grandeur of Kemiraj is, as they say, peerless. I'm glad that you summoned me here, for back in the capital I had hardly anything to do. Idleness doesn't suit me."

"And here I thought you were about to say that you missed me."

Nuawa gets small glimpses of the city-layers below as they cross the station: a trapezoid of walkways here, a triangle of market there, each brightly lit and dyed. A city that defies nature. "I'm saving that for later, General."

They climb into the carriage, a sleek vehicle done in dark wood and fecund upholstery, its engine nearly silent. Nuawa sits close to the general, for all that there is plenty of space to go between them. She runs her finger along the paneling, feels the faint thrum of ghosts, though her eyes are always on Lussadh.

The general puts a hand on the base of her spine, lightly. "There's something about you," Lussadh says, turning her around and kissing her.

Each time they are apart, Nuawa would think she has had her fill: lust is basal, but it can be resisted, put aside. But the general's mouth, there is sweetness to it and heat, compelling, even addicting. She undoes her jacket so Lussadh can bite her throat and unbuttons her shirt so Lussadh can lick her breast. A vivid image takes hold of her, of straddling and taking the general inside her, and as the wheels run over ruts the carriage would jolt Lussadh deeper into her.

The carriage does judder, but to a stop. Lussadh lets go. "My apologies. I forgot the ride was so short. You make me forget so much so easily."

Nuawa quickly corrects her state of undress. Her nipples are hard and tender. "On the contrary you forget nothing at all," she says, a little breathy. "After having your mouth all over me, I can't imagine ever feeling cold again."

"How delightful to hear from a woman ten years younger than I."

"Who's to say I have not always pursued older partners? The wealth of experience." She looks up at the general through her eyelashes. "The mastery."

Lussadh grins like a cat and Nuawa thinks how easy it is to fall into the role, this role. Not one she ever imagined she must don, yet it is effortless.

Disembarking they are saluted by soldiers wearing the same uniforms they are, black and gray and silver, the uniform Nuawa never dreamed of wearing either. It too fits well, she moves with ease in it, the tailoring very fine as befits the queen's own. She wonders how the other glass-bearers react to this, the elevation from common gladiator to one of the most powerful officers in winter.

The palace is not situated at the highest point of Kemiraj; rather it is central, mounted on an artificial hill at the heart of an eight-pointed star. Four minarets rise over the expanse of stone and glass. Each tower is in the shade of turquoise, citrine, sunstone, padparadscha. From this distance Nuawa can't tell if they are walled in semi-precious gems or merely painted stone, but they look enough like it, impossibly expensive.

In the palace, walls and doors shift open at Lussadh's approach, seal themselves shut once she has passed. The ceiling is impossibly distant, as though these hallways have been made to deific scale, an abode for deva to fill with their celestial breath and celestial footfalls. Lanterns cascade from wall sconces like grapes; lights spin in them, rose-gold and silver, in the manner of intoxicated fireflies. Non-military staff have already been restored—many of the personnel bow rather than salute, and at a glance she judges them to be noncombatants, not just from their presentation but the way they carry themselves. She spots a couple thaumaturges she's seen before back in the capital and a few clerks she suspects are intelligence operatives or assassins. They're always about, part of Lussadh's retinue.

"This is my apartment when I'm in residence," Lussadh is saying as they enter a palace wing guarded by a high gate wrapped in thorns. "The bathhouse is separate, over in the gardens. We can share a bedroom or not. I leave to you the choice."

"After the carriage, I'd never deny myself that joy. And did you not call me here so we could wake up beside one another?"

Lussadh laughs and ushers her into the suite. The general's quarters take up half the wing: rooms joined by twisting convex corridors, by alcoves inlaid with zircons and robed in shadow. There are slit-narrow windows, and there are ones broad and curved to fit two walls so that one can gaze out upon Kemiraj in full—a vertiginous view of latticework balconies, honeycomb pavilions, and bromeliad gardens. These are quarters grander than the queen's, and this is a city more splendid than the capital. Despite herself, Nuawa stands by the window, exhaling on the pane. "I've never seen anything like this."

"Life should be full of marvels. I've always wanted to show you my home." The general pecks her on the ear.

They unpack. The general lays out her clothes—getting a good look at her weapons in the process, not that Nuawa has anything to hide—and unfolds the diptych, putting it in a corner next to frothing potted plants. Lussadh does not remark upon it, having acclimated to its presence in their shared room back in the capital, the diptych of a painted forever sky and incandescent colors. A world in which it is always summer.

She takes off her coat, then slides off Lussadh's. Her hand hovering over the general's bicep, she says, "Who wounded you?"

"An enemy soldier. That happens."

"May I look?"

There is a pause. "Yes."

She thinks of the queen peeling the snakeskin off Vahatma, an act of unveiling something divine and dangerous, and she does likewise. Each article of clothing she removes from Lussadh with that same languor, that same force of intent. She puts her hand down the general's chest, over skin like embersilk and muscles like chiseled bronze. "Do you get tired of being told you are breathtaking, General?" The wound is hidden behind gauze, but she can see that it is like a crater, not made by something as neat as a bullet or even an arrow. "Yet it feels impossible to deny that you are. It feels impossible to say you're anything less than superb." She traces long, meandering lines around the site of injury.

"No virtue or effort of my own. My grandaunt the king selected—and bred—her potential heirs for many advantages, beauty among them. I was part of a batch; we all had a particular look." The general catches her hand, pulling her glove off. Kisses her knuckles, one by one. "We're getting distracted again, aren't we? I have to brief you. The queen let me know of this engineer she wishes to ... commission."

Nuawa slides off her other glove. "Penjarej Manachakul is hiding here under a different name, I assume. I don't know how she met Ytoba, or why she passed her rather esoteric knowledge on. It'd be helpful if ey had sketched us an image of the professor, but ey wasn't so obliging."

Lussadh's features tighten, minutely. "Ey is dead."

"I saw to it. The head I burned. The rest I separated—the governor of Kavaphat was visiting, and her tigers eat anything." She watches for any further opening, any sign, but the general betrays nothing else. "Do you suppose our engineer is still alive? After all this turmoil."

"We'll have to bet on the professor being a survivor. That does seem to be the way of your city."

Such a remark can mean anything. Nuawa chooses to take note but not dwell.

They go over ways through which a person might disappear, trace the paths Penjarej Manachakul might have taken to obfuscate her origins and identity. It is the closest to a precipice she has ever been since the tribute tournament, for though the professor is unlikely to have used the same methods as Mother Indrahi, still this strikes close to home. But Indrahi was a spymaster in her time; she knew how to disappear, and she hid who she had been to the end. Hid herself, hid Nuawa, hid even her estranged son behind the saffron robe.

"Nuawa?"

She must have allowed this line of thought to show. She swallows down the clotting weight, the hot press of grief. It will not do. Her mother raised her better than this. "I was thinking on whether Ytoba could have taught her to alter her shape in return for her expertise. Is that possible?"

Lussadh blinks and straightens. "Hah. Fortunately for us, no. It can't be taught, more a discipline struck deep into the flesh before birth. A hundred modifications of the skin and bone, and a hundred more when the shapeshifter reaches a certain age. Surgeries throughout their first ten, fifteen years of life."

"It doesn't sound pleasant."

"It wasn't; I watched children screaming under knives and flensing shadows, I watched their stomachs inverted and poured out. Kemiraj assassins are—were—a sect of their own. Conditioned to zealotry before they learned to talk, loyal to the throne because this purpose was all they had. Abolishing their order was one of the first things I did. So many orphans they'd taken in, so many mouths parents couldn't afford to feed. There were babies left in the dunes to feed the wind-lynxes. King Ihsayn thought it a sensible arrangement. The children would have died regardless, and the sect paid the parents well."

"Were they grateful? The children you freed."

The general draws out another roll of paper, one that records recent arrivals to Kemiraj. "The ones old enough to talk cursed my name, called me the al-Kattan seed gone to rot, and prophesied my doom. They'd be adults now, perhaps raising children of their own. I wonder if Ytoba ever returned to any of them in eir years of hiding, to stoke that fire, if there's anything more than ashes remaining."

One end of the paper curls, unruly. Nuawa weighs it down with a samovar. "We will find out, General. And I'm glad to be here, to see at last the land of your nativity." To behold and taste the country that birthed this creature before her, and perhaps to understand how monsters—like Nuawa herself—are made.

THREE

THE IMMIGRATION OFFICE occupies a building of its own, one of the many adjunct compounds that share a platform with the palace. From the outside it is boxy, plain; from the inside it is cavernous, a few small rooms partitioned off for entrance and exit interviews, countless mezzanines overhead bearing countless typewriters. Paper spills from cabinets and workstations, sheets neat and crumpled, shreds on the floor and peeking from between a typewriter's maw. Nuawa moves her handlamp across the gloom, its beam falling on dust and girders. The building's ghosts have been shut down or released, leaving the light-bulbs dead, the typewriters and behemoth printing presses in hibernation.

On one of the mezzanines, three of Ulamat's clerks are sorting loose documents and exhuming folders from the cabinets. Volumes of departures and arrivals, residences granted and denied, registries of addresses and workplaces. They are efficient, the clerks, though watching them convinces Nuawa more than ever that this is a recreation of hell. An afterlife reserved for corrupt officials, destined to forever stack up and file and order paperwork that'd then be scattered anew.

On his part, Ulamat is surveying one of the many shelves and feeding tar-dark ghosts to a typewriter. Pulling a few levers, he coaxes the machine to reproduce the last thing it typed; it does with a guttering, metallic noise. "Ah," he says, "this ought to be helpful."

"A tidy trick." Nuawa crosses the floor, cupping her hand around her handlamp to direct its light. "You're exceedingly skilled. Not everyone can fight, spy, and tinker around with logic machines. And to do all of them well."

He gives her a smile halved by shadow and lamplight. "I was born of the enamel. In Kemiraj that carries a particular meaning. The prince selected me for salvation, and to her I owe everything—my education, my standing, my life. From her I've seen more kindness than from my own elders. In a place like mine, Lieutenant, one learns to be useful."

She does not know what it means to be enamel-born in Kemiraj. But it does trouble her that Ulamat accepted his lot, was trained into grateful obedience. Of course, the general has shown him more kindness than his own kin, who could hardly afford to clothe and feed him as well as a prince could. For Lussadh, funding a deprived child cost her nothing. "Your loyalty to her is exemplary."

The aide continues to smile. "I strive to keep it so. We should have the information you need in a day or two. It ought to be straightforward enough—Magistrate Sareha had no reason to hide Professor Penjarej. We'll keep an eye out too for recent deaths, though those aren't always registered, and obituaries are for those with means. Still, a few days. My people are good at what they do."

It is a dismissal, however polite: she is in the way, having herself no skill with paperwork and archives. There is a distance. Odd, for when they last saw each other Ulamat was pleasant, made small talk, asked her about her dueling career—even professed himself a fan. "I trust you with your work, Ulamat. Is there a temple in Kemiraj that serves those of my faith?"

"The Seven Spires. It's a collective house of worship but they have Sirapirat monks, an extensive ecclesiastic collection." He hands her a map.

"The priests, are they under house arrest?"

"As all civilians are. The general will transition them to a loose curfew soon. It's not good to keep citizens holed up in their homes too long." He stretches and moves to the next typewriter, casting a glance at the filing station where more volumes and loose papers await. "In point of fact, there are members of the clergy to whom Magistrate Sareha shared confidences, among the shrine-keepers of Kidashoten. I've already been at the Spires incognito, but the presence of an officer might smoke someone out."

Perhaps he means to see whether she's willing to rough up a few holy bodies, whether in white or saffron. "Let the general know I'll be out." She gathers her coat and furs, not that she needs them in a climate so warm. Habit wins out.

The boulevards of Kemiraj are wide, two lanes given to vehicles, the other two to stalls that must have until recently hosted street vendors. A thin sheen of ice rims the windows and street signs, clinging in curlicues to lamp posts and eaves, to the long-limbed fruit-less trees that must have been transplanted from far away. They have generous, heart-shaped leaves shot through with silver capillaries, traces of lavender and pink.

The queen's image laces the air. Her face on the facade of a building, her crown in the banners that fly and snap in nearly every corner, monuments at each gate in her likeness: larger than life, carved of blue-white stone, with metal torques at arms and thighs, a sword-scepter in hand. Her bathyal gaze from high above, remorseless and omniscient. But having abided in the palace, where the genuine article is present and much more literal, Nuawa does not feel as suffocated by the queen's image as she once did. She catches a reflection of herself in a storefront; even wrapped up as she is, she is obliged to display the hyacinth. The things one gets used to, one compromise at a time.

An ache pulses in her abdomen, a warning. She finds a secluded corner between two stalls—both have tables, stained by spilled coconut milk and curry—and takes out the ivory case her Sirapirat chiurgeon gave her. One breath she draws, then another, waiting for the pain to rise. The medication is the one belonging she will not part with, for she has to take it twice a day to suppress the parasite she willingly hosts. *By next year it'll be a part of you and removing it will be fatal,* her chiurgeon warned. *By year five it'll kill you dead, messily, and it'll be pure agony leading up to that. Is that what you want?* Five years: a deadline she's imposed on herself to strive against the queen, though in the meantime the parasite shields her from malicious thaumaturgy, poison, etheric wear and tear. She's tested it against a few common toxins and so far the parasite has absorbed every one. A fair exchange.

Inside their case, the pills are bright yellow, tinged orange at the center. She dry-swallows one and screws the case shut. In a few months she will run out and need an alchemist willing to produce more of this for her or return to Sirapirat for a refill. Or perhaps in a few months she will be dead and no longer need any of these.

A haze pulls over her vision. Everything becomes silicate structure, translucent and perfectly geometric: the back of her hand is all bones, licked by frost. It passes and she is flesh again. She rubs at her eyes. This is not a side-effect her chiurgeon ever mentioned, but it's been happening lately, some symptom of the parasite unaccounted for.

The boulevard splits, one leading to a bridge that climbs, another to a ramp that slants below. Nuawa consults the map: it is well-illustrated and crisp, but it assumes familiarity with Kemiraj that she doesn't have. Landmarks are foregrounded, enlarged to the point they eclipse pathways, and it leaves the level ambiguous. The Seven Spires could be above or below her.

She goes down. The ramp is of darker, grainier stone and the buildings soon turn less manicured, their facades more papered: week-old broadsheets, laminated posters for theatrical productions and music and inventors' fairs. They are of a higher quality than seen elsewhere, but she's heading into a less refined part of the city and therefore almost certainly the wrong direction. Unlike Sirapirat, this is a city—she suspects—where the houses of worship congregate in a certain kind of neighborhood. She keeps on, nevertheless. It intrigues her to see what poverty might look like in this jeweled territory.

The stalls grow denser, the footpaths more crowded with extensions from teahouses—tables and benches, small canopies to shade from the sunlight. What sunlight it is: she's never seen day so bright as in Kemiraj, and she thinks back to the oneiric visions Ytoba brought her in the arena, from when this land was still a desert. Even the queen cannot entirely dim this brilliance.

Even the queen cannot reshape the world's laws completely.

"Absolute winter," Nuawa says under her breath and laughs, a dry, dead-leaf sound.

She walks past houses leaning close, under the tidiest laundry lines she has ever seen. The curtains twitch and faces peer out, but they quickly disappear. Not a single window is crooked and at nearly every door there are potted bromeliads, berry shrubs red or purple with fruit. The latter most of all catches her by surprise. In Sirapirat, being able to keep fruit-bearing plants—outside greenhouses, no less— would be the mark of considerable wealth.

By and by she circles back to the Seven Spires. A pair of soldiers guard the gate, a construction of bright iron and sheened ivory. The compound is nothing like the rest of Kemiraj, new and foreign, the queen's clearest handprint on the city. Tiered, wooden roofs painted in jade green and black and red, individual shrines with papered doors and bells in each god's colors. The walls are high but bare, absent the naga with which Nuawa is familiar, those gilded heads and silver fangs.

Of all the shrines, Kidashoten's is the greatest, twice as tall as the rest and three times as wide. The ceiling is strung with paper talismans, wishes and prayers, in gray or indigo according to its taxonomy. Kidashoten's statue rears on a plinth, one bare ankle haloed in candlelight. Wings grow from their back, their limbs, their flanks and hips; in place of hair, filoplumes and pinions sprout. There is more than a passing resemblance, Nuawa notices, between the god and the snow-girls. The cut of the features, the lightness of figure. She does not leave offerings.

More than a few times she catches sight of a temple janitor, layperson by the look of them, full-figured and compactly made. Much darker than Lussadh, a native of Johramu perhaps. They keep their gaze down, but there's something to their bearing, a certain sharpness. Nuawa takes note but keeps to her course.

She locates the monks' scriptorium; its signpost is in Ughali rather than the local Mehrut script. Entering she takes off her boots and adjusts her hyacinth, making sure it rides high and prominent on her shoulder. Such a delicate symbol for such unparalleled tyranny. A novice in sandstone robes greets her. She tells them that she wishes to speak to the senior bhikkuni or monk.

The novice ushers her through the prayer auditorium, where a statue of the Great Teacher sits beneath a tree of slow-moving hands noisily animated by clockwork. No ghost engine here, other than the central heating shared with the rest of the Seven Spires. The senior bhikkuni Kabilsingh receives her behind a screen of lotuses, nodding at Nuawa, not quite a bow—lieutenant or not, Nuawa is a layperson— and gestures at the floor. "How might I offer you succor, seeker?"

Nuawa lowers herself, folding her knees. It is habit: a bhikkuni or monk sits elevated, a layperson on the ground. She gives obeisance thrice. Whatever else, she was not raised to be a barbarian. "I'm far from home. This is my first assignment abroad and there's much to miss. Familiar sights, familiar food, familiar people."

Kabilsingh's smile is framed by deep, etched creases. Her vestments are thick embersilk and lamellar plates, almost like armor. "I believe I know who you are. I was born in Sirapirat and was part of Wat Totsanee some eight years ago, ten now maybe. Your victory in the games was broadcast. It's not often—indeed never—that I see a child of our city wearing the queen's flower."

Without missing a beat Nuawa says, "And I hope to do Sirapirat proud."

"Being the first can be a terrible burden." The bhikkuni studies her. "Or a rare opportunity. Kemiraj is a city of transplants, and many from Sirapirat came here in search of work they couldn't have found back home. I can point you to where most of them live, seeker, if community will soothe your spirit and give you solace in this foreign land."

There's negotiation in this offer: even the holy look for privileges. And the scriptorium, she expects, isn't as well-funded as the rest of the Spires. "I'd be grateful for that. And my apologies that I brought no suitable offerings—I was reared better than this, truly. I'll rectify it when I come next time." Hinting that if Kabilsingh can direct her to Penjarej, the scriptorium might see a sudden large donation.

On the way out, Nuawa does another circuit of the Seven Spires. So much green, so much color, long-leafed shrubs and slender aspens. Yellow winter aconites, glittering snowdrops, flushed cyclamens. It represents unthinkable luxury, even for a favored house of worship.

Between the plants rise statues of Kidashoten's attendants, white birds with six or seven wings each. A religion of the sky.

Nuawa goes wide around a corner, a practice she maintains to keep from being surprised. Sure enough: the janitor has taken advantage of that corner, lying in wait. She draws her gun.

"Wait." The janitor holds up their empty hands. They flick their wrist and the queen's hyacinth materializes, nestled in their palm. "You nearly made me blow my cover. I'm Guryin. Major Guryin, but we mustn't sweat the titles."

Nuawa holsters her sidearm. "Absolute winter," she says, though she wishes she could keep the pistol out.

"Exactly. Let's take this elsewhere, shall we?"

They adjourn to a carriage in the back of the Seven Spires, a black vehicle without insignias, but which passes through the guards without drawing comment. Once inside Guryin takes off xer shabby outer coat and lets down xer long, thick hair. "What a relief. Being incognito is much less glamorous than you'd think, you wouldn't believe *where* dead leaves or incense dust can end up. You're Nuawa, yes? Lieutenant Nuawa Dasaret?"

"Yes. I have heard much about you, Major." She hasn't actually, but Lussadh has spoken of the other glass-bearers here and there, enough that she knows how to address Guryin. "If I may ask, why were you undercover?"

"To lend you a hand, of course. And if *I* may say, what were you doing?"

The carriage bumps against a rare rough patch in the road. They are approaching a checkpoint: two mobile barricades, a staff of two soldiers and a sniper stationed above, on the second floor of a nearby glassblower's. "Sending out feelers. Sirapirat immigrants, religious or not, gather at temples. It's a social habit of ours, Major, and I would either be introduced to my target or spook her into doing something foolish and therefore exposing herself."

Xe tosses xer head and laughs, full-throated. "You sound like you know what you're doing—not bad, even if your methods are like sledgehammers. I'd feared you would be less ... thoughtful. But the general would never take a dull person to bed."

She glances sideways, at Guryin and at the seat divider that sepa-
rates them. Behind the major, the carriage's small round window
shows a wall rushing by, clad in a lace of black ice. "I wasn't aware it
was such public knowledge." It is not that she believed Lussadh would
keep her a secret, but she thought these things would be more private.

"It's not like that. Only that we know each other's business. Us
glass-bearers, we're like a family. Have you met everyone yet? No? Not
my betrothed Colonel Imsou either? They're one of us, runs Johramu
—anyway, Lussadh has never taken a lover among our own, and it's so
much healthier this way. To be able to share everything with your
companion, all that mystical mirror business. And she has been single
for so long."

Nuawa catches a whiff of frankincense and lemongrass, and under
those a hint of something bitter, vinegary. Thaumaturges often smell
like that—substances of the ether can leave behind a distinct scent,
rarely pleasant—and wear fragrances to cover up the fact. "She is the
queen's consort."

Guryin pops open one of the carriage's compartments and
rummages through it before producing, inexplicably, a bouquet of
fabric flowers. Xe plucks out a surprisingly lifelike rose, bright yellow
fading to white at the edges. "You are not jealous, I hope? Good." Xe
turns the rose over to her, closing her fingers around the wire-and-
velvet stem. "Now, yes, there is the queen. What Lussadh does with
her is like prayer or divine communion. What I do with Imsou is
taking each other to plays or operas, sparring, decorating each other's
room. I cook their favorite dishes and when they come across a rare
book I want, they bring it back as a gift. Love isn't transcendent sex
with an elemental force. Love is the small things, the company, the
shared moments. The everyday."

And, she supposes, the queen does not stoop to the everyday.
"This is a lot of information to hand out to a stranger you've just met,
Major."

"But we are no strangers! We share a common bond. You may call
me older-sibling. I have decided that I like you." Guryin claps xer
hands. "I know just what you could get Lussadh. She loves anthuri-

ums. Really the only flower she enjoys. Ah, we're back. Let's go see the general together so I can make her introduce us properly."

————

IN THE MORNING-DAPPLED THRONE HALL, Lussadh stands by the dais and it is as if time has not passed at all and nothing has changed: she is sixteen again, waiting on King Ihsayn. Even the faces before her —bent, their brows against the floor—have not changed much. A handful were old courtiers, old commanders who pledged themselves to her as she plotted her coup in those long nights, before the dawn of frost and slaughter. She'd traded promises, whispered a vision, one in which their place in the world would no longer depend on their lineage and proximity to the al-Kattan: a scout from Shuriam could become a captain, an enamel-born clerk could become a magistrate. It meant something, that they had sworn their fealty to her and broken their oath to the king, but then she had thought Sareha loyal for decades.

There is no surety, and the ground underneath her is quicksand: the softness of history, the drowning pull.

Those gathered know her and so they do not look up, they do not plead their innocence or reassert their allegiance. She looks from head to head, most disheveled and matted with sweat. They were trapped when she shut down the palace, in rooms and offices, one or two in the baths. For the entirety of the siege they were stranded. Two weeks. By the time Lussadh released the palace's doors and walls there were a dozen bodies, some of them children of officials who brought their households there. Again, she scans the faces: officials that have lost their children are not in attendance. Altogether the crowd before her is twenty-five, the highest-ranking among commanders and councilors that survived. All are weak with starvation, tremulous with fear.

"Thank you for coming," Lussadh says. The kind of politeness Ihsayn would have scoffed at. *You shall be king, and a king commands.* "All of you must be weary. Sareha's treason was unmatched in scale or cruelty. She knew what would happen to you and did not stop to care."

Shifting the weight, assigning fault to the dead. "Be on your knees or your feet, as suits your strength."

A ripple of jerky motion as they pull themselves upright, tired joints popping. She surveys their haggard faces and finds only the expected reactions—fear, uncertainty, mouths bent and jawlines tight. "My first priority," she says, and can almost feel on her back the gaze of the dead king, the throne-haunt, "will be order. Kemiraj is an immense, breathing thing, and I will not have martial law drag on needlessly. Curfew will be eased piecemeal, and your offices will be reinstated as swiftly as possible. I will want your opinion on which part of the city requires immediate attention."

They blink at her, startled. A few mouths twitch in disbelief. Their bodies have been tensed, the language of those bracing for retribution. "My lord," the Minister of Commerce begins and stops herself.

"Minister Veshma." Lussadh gestures at one of her most senior ministers—part of the cadre that's been with her since Ihsayn's fall—and wonders if Veshma's head, too, will need to roll. Only death suffices to clear a name: to not have survived Sareha's coup is the sole functional proof of innocence. "I'm fond of your feasts and you've always been a fine host. Arrange a reception worthy of my return to Kemiraj. The guest list I'll leave to you." For that itself can be as telling as anything. "Captain Juhye, I have a new officer, Lieutenant Nuawa Dasaret. She is unfamiliar with military service. Lieutenant Nuawa will have her own duties, but when your time and hers coincide I'd like her to learn from you."

"Sir." He salutes, clenched fist over heart, as sharply as though he's been hale rather than famished for half a month.

"The rest of you I will speak with in due course."

Veshma stays behind. The minister gives her a deep curtsy, the gesture compliant with old mores. Most of Kemiraj will never stop thinking of her as their prince.

"Go on," Lussadh says. "Though you should get something to eat."

"That can wait, my lord." The minister's hands shake from hunger. "The feast you would have me prepare. How wide should I cast the nets?"

Bargaining and seeking a position of trust, or perhaps Veshma wishes to avoid having the guest list be a test of herself. "Very wide. Of everyone who survived, pick whoever you think would be good company, civilian or military. I'll foot the expenses."

"The city entire would come if it could. Kemiraj has missed you, my lord, especially those of us who had the privilege of watching you grow. All of us yearn to see you more often in residence, in this country that is our shared heart." The minister looks as if she might say something more, but she merely bows a second time.

On her way out she nearly collides with Major Guryin who—as is xer wont—has not bothered to announce xerself. Xe catches and gallantly steadies Veshma before sending the minister off with a roguish wink. Then xe takes Nuawa's hand like a dance partner and pushes her forward. "General, I deliver to your keeping a rare beauty, elegant as a talwar, scintillating as a leopard. Finally, you've picked someone you can be seen in public with!" Xe gives Nuawa a mean-ingful glance. "I kept throwing lovely prospects at her and she turned every last one down. Really picky."

"Guryin," Lussadh begins. Sighs. "What was it—an islander princess, yes, that would've been a diplomatic disaster and she was besotted with you, actually. Then the marquess, who I think even you didn't like."

"My liking is not the point. You never put in any real effort, and your own selections don't usually last even a week." Guryin claps Nuawa on the back, vigorous enough for the impact to resound gunfire-like across the hall. On her part the lieutenant absorbs the blow and keeps her footing, expression unchanging. "Shame on you for not throwing a party and bringing us all together to meet her."

"A grave faux pas that I'll rectify when the time is right. How did you two run into each other?"

"The Seven Spires—Lieutenant Nuawa here is very spiritual." Xe beams. "I've got a few loose ends out there but couldn't miss an opportunity to meet our newest addition. I'll report back. Now I leave you two; goodness knows when my betrothed and I were new to one another we hated a third wheel."

Guryin leaves humming, waving to both of them.

"Major Guryin is very disarming." Nuawa gazes after Guryin's passage. "I asked xer what exactly xe was doing in the Spires and only now do I realize xe never did quite answer. Xe seems apt to charm the pelt off a wolf, the scales off a cobra."

"Yet not much off you, I suspect." Lussadh turns to the table on which she has spread a map out like a cadaver, the anatomy of a city gutted open and laid bare. It is one of the most detailed of Kemiraj, almost a schematic. "Xe is a skilled infiltrator." She doesn't say that xe has been infiltrating districts where Sirapirat transplants concentrate, partly to find Professor Penjarej, partly to guard against Nuawa. Such things will make themselves evident to the lieutenant as needed.

The lieutenant pushes herself onto the table, loosely perching. "The major invited me to call xer older-sibling. Are all glass-bearers like this?"

Lussadh notes, on reflex, that while Nuawa wears her blade openly she keeps the gun in a concealed holster, under the jacket. To not scare the monks, or simply duelist habit. "Not at all. Guryin is one of a kind. Xe's right, though, that I ought to make the introductions. There are six of us, an exclusive fellowship."

Nuawa runs her fingers along the edge of the map, thumb poised on the junction where paper meets mosaic. There is an odd refinement to even this loose stance, and Lussadh thinks—as she thought when she first saw Nuawa—this is what animated calligraphy might be, all numinous lines. "Do you kiss every glass-bearer on sight, General? To ascertain what we are."

"Certainly not." She raises an eyebrow. "It doesn't always manifest that way, and I'm not always attracted. You were an unusual case; I'd never felt the pull as strong."

"Ah." It is a long and contemplative sound. "I don't entirely understand it. You've not told me much of what the mirror shards do to us." She presses the heel of her palm to her breast, as if to feel for the cold glass inside, that sliver of puissance.

Lussadh looks on, struck by this gesture, desire tightening her blood. There is no innocence to Nuawa, but there is that quality of pristineness, of a being above the toil and reek of mortal life. "You don't get pneumonia or hypothermia. Your flesh is strengthened in small but definite ways, and so is your reason. The shard banks the fire of emotions that make us weak, like fear or panic or confusion. Glass-bearers know resolve as total as mountains." And the mirror makes it impossible for any bearer to turn against the queen, a fact only she and the queen know. A slight alteration of nature, one that makes previous allegiance or political leaning irrelevant, and which bends the bearer's actions—conscious or not—to the queen's desires. But it does not necessarily prevent Nuawa from acting against another glass-bearer. In this isolate moment Lussadh imagines throwing Nuawa to the floor and shooting her in the head for treachery, and she finds that she is able to hold this in her mind even though it is a jagged, biting thing.

"A tremendous gift, and here I was ignorant of it my entire life." Nuawa passes her hand along a loose knot of gray print on the map that represents a bridge nexus. "I've approached someone that might be able to produce Professor Penjarej, or at least cause her to slip up and show herself. Do I have leave to act freely?"

"I trust your judgment." Lussadh pauses. "Though I'll expect you to get acquainted with one of my officers. Captain Juhye's an old soldier of mine, and I want him watched. The pretext of having him train you in protocols is as good as any."

"I'll keep an eye on him. And—" The lieutenant hesitates. "Do you think love is in the everyday? The small things."

Lussadh opens her mouth and closes it, caught off-guard. "It's one way of defining that, certainly. I have not given it much thought, and not in those terms. Why?"

"Nothing, General." Nuawa turns her gaze to the table mosaic, lifting a corner of the map to peer underneath, at the lapis lazuli tiles arranged into an image of the queen. "It was merely a notion."

FOUR

THE MORNING before Veshma's feast, Lussadh lifts the curfew and arranges for every restaurant, eatery and teahouse in the city to throw wide their doors. "For three days," she tells Ulamat, "they are to feed anyone who comes through their doors, from sunup to sundown. Have them spread their seating out onto the footpaths. Requisition spare furniture for them—we've always got more stools and canopies than we can use."

"This will be costly, my lord." He adjusts his spectacles and turns the page on his ledger, tapping it with his pen. "But well within our means. A few months ago, we confiscated an occidental merchant's cargo of considerable volume. He was drunk, mistook one of your officers for a courtesan, and vulgarly propositioned her; the merchant's since been barred from entering winter territories. Among the inventory were exotic grains, minor jewelry, and foreign coinage. Do I have your leave to distribute these to hospital staff and municipal workers?"

By which he means laborers, janitors, the poorly-paid and most of them enamel-born. To such people luxurious goods can sometimes be bartered more effectively than simple currency. "You have my leave. Sareha's estate is getting expropriated and I'll sign her liquid assets over to you. Make use of them as you will." A stipend for the most junior civil servants and infantry, a few debts bought out and a few lives unburdened. Many children of the enamel forget their roots; Ulamat never does.

Lussadh glances at her watch: the hour is about right. She returns to her apartment to see that the tailor she commissioned is already there. He is a round-hipped man with long, quick fingers, and he is currently measuring the lieutenant's shoulders with a tape. "Stunning proportions, sir," he is exclaiming when Lussadh enters, jotting down abbreviations and numbers into a pad in his hand. "That of a master-work! Flattering your figure will be simplicity itself. Does the lieutenant have any particular preferences?"

"Pockets. The dress uniform has a coat, as I understand. I'll want something that can seamlessly hide a holster." Nuawa stands with arms spread scarecrow-wide. She looks up past the tailor and meets Lussadh's gaze with an embarrassed shrug. "Comfortable collars. Little metallic thread, no sequins, no seed pearls. Actually, no paillette at all if you can help it."

The tailor snaps his measuring tape shut, puts his little notebook back into a pocket. "Ah, a person of minimalist taste. As you wish, sir." He turns to Lussadh and drops to his knees. "Lord-Governor! I did the preliminary work yesterday and it is short notice, but it shall be ready within two hours."

"Plenty of time. I trust your work." Lussadh gestures at him to rise. "Are you about finished here?"

"Indeed, lord. I shall send the result and hope my utmost that the lieutenant will be pleased. Absolute winter, sirs." He enunciates this sharply, importantly, as if the phrase includes him in the governing and administering of the queen's reign. He curtsies his way out.

Nuawa shakes her head as she buttons up her shirt. "I keep forgetting that *sir* in Mehrut is different from ... the equivalent in Ughali. Not that we have an equivalent, exactly. Is this not excessive, General? I can wear my normal uniform."

"It's a tense time and dressing up redirects people's anxieties. I need something to lance the boil, so to speak, and need it fast. The reception will serve many purposes, and the drinks will loosen many tongues. With what I've decreed in the city at large, the people will make their own festivities. Regardless of what Sareha's left behind, subversive elements have a hard time breeding when the populace isn't immediately discontented." Lussadh bolts the door. Her eyes fall, by accident, on the diptych Nuawa brings with her everywhere. The saturated colors that coat the canvas and make all else beside it seem bleached, thin.

"Statecraft sounds implosively complex."

"Implosive, yes. Complex, no—merely a matter of logistics. Much of it can be dealt with systematically; courtiers, ministers, and military officers are predictable in their own ways. Each average citizen may have unique concerns and impulses, but in the collective they are easily anticipated, like herd animals." She kneels behind the divan Nuawa occupies, putting her face level with the lieutenant's. "That includes me. My grandaunt believed that the king is above and apart, that the ruler is not integrated into the collective organ. In that, as in much else, she was incorrect."

Nuawa turns around and reaches over, hooking Lussadh's hair behind her ear. "You're no herd animal."

"No?"

"Too soft and wooly, and far too herbivorous. You're omnivorous in every sense, with a great preference for meat. Let me see." Nuawa snaps her fingers. "Vampire bats are social—"

Lussadh snorts. "You're comparing me to flying rodents?"

"Something grander, then. Certain seals are polygamous, and I believe certain tigers form harems around the most powerful member of the pack. That ought to suit you better."

"Now I'm an aquatic cow, then a large cat. Will your insults never cease?" She vaults over the divan, landing atop and loosely straddling Nuawa. "What will it be next, baboons?"

"Since I've got you on top of me, it appears insulting you cease-lessly leads to a most rewarding result." The lieutenant widens her eyes, one hand cupping Lussadh's hip. "Tiger it is—all carnivorous habits and glorious teeth and mighty claws. Which you can now demonstrate upon me ..."

And she is well enticed: it is hard not to be, with Nuawa lying soft and warm under her, one of Nuawa's knees sliding up between her thighs. To kiss that mouth until it swells. "Don't think I do not want to." She passes her hand down Nuawa's front, brushing over stomach, over breasts. "But the feast impends, and we must both prepare, keep our wits about us. You, my lieutenant, have a deleterious effect on mine."

The lieutenant laughs as they get up together, but quickly arranges her expression into one of mock solemnity. "Very well, General. Shall I go to the party as your bodyguard or your arm decoration?"

Lussadh clicks her tongue and straightens out Nuawa's collars. "You're no mere ornament." Her finger grazes a collarbone, its velvet invitation; she pulls her hand back swiftly before temptation can take hold of her again. Not everything she has said to the lieutenant is lover's flattery—there *is* a pull, one as elemental as magnetism. "Officially you'll be introduced as my new protégé, to be treated much as other glass-bearers are, though of course they don't know what the hyacinth *means*." To the public it serves simply as a mark of the queen's favor; the truth of the mirror is classified. "Commanders will wish to make your acquaintance. Captain Juhye particularly. Kemiraj's court will likewise seek your attention."

"To see where I fit in the hierarchy, how I might be utilized or circumvented."

"You've got a dim view of courtiers. Though not wrong." She holds up her fingers, ticking them off. "For comportment you've nothing to worry about, your table manners are elegant, your composure is total. Can you hold your liquor?"

Nuawa pours herself the lukewarm tisane a servant has left behind. She inhales the combined scents of tamarind and honey. "I promise not to faint into your arms or vomit on your shoes."

"I'll hold you to that. Because this is the first time in two years that I have returned to Kemiraj and the circumstances are unique, I will be going further than I usually do to draw people out. As much as I remind them that I'm no longer ..." Royalty, a prince, a king-in-waiting. "No longer what I used to be, habits are like religion. I remain unmarried; that leaves a vacuum."

"The real reason I cannot decorate your arm." The lieutenant's mouth twitches into a smirk. "Will I get to watch you flirt with beautiful women? Outfitted like butterflies, in brilliant dancing shoes, gazing longingly into your eyes. I shall hire poets to commemorate it."

"You sound absolutely entertained." Lussadh nudges the lieutenant lightly on the nose. "Keep going and I'll send some of those your way. There will be a variety—the daughters of ministers, newly minted officers, ambitious inventors and scholars. Perhaps you'll like the intellectuals best? No reason for me to hog all the attention."

"Major Guryin will be upset to miss this," Nuawa says, deadpan. "The event will be too exclusive for Penjarej Manachakul to show up, won't it?"

"The guest list doesn't include her name, so either she's living in obscurity or she is a prominent inventor but using an alias. But if she was prominent enough to rate Veshma's regard, I would have known of her—not too many Sirapirat in Kemiraj." None prominent, politically or otherwise. Sirapirat is considered provincial.

The lieutenant's expression flickers, for the tiniest instant. Then she says, "All to the good, General. As the only Sirapirat there, I shall be most exotic at the ball, and lovely women may drift my way despite everything."

———

THE CLOTHES ARRIVE EARLY, and despite Nuawa's reservations, her dress uniform is a perfect fit. Like the field uniform, it is in black, gray, silver. But the outer coat is layered, with wide, long sleeves that fall nearly to the ground, in the same style as the queen's brocade robes. No belt: instead a wide sash, pale gray, to pull tight across the coat. Moving around in it, Nuawa finds the sleeves close to impossible to deal with, though the width does hide the holster she straps to her arm.

On her part, the general does not bother with a uniform: she dresses simply as herself. The top half of her dress is a structured jacket that bares her throat and upper chest, foregrounding the hyacinth she wears on a pendant—the only symbol of her rank, other than the fact that she wears her weapons openly. The dress flows into a tapered skirt, slit nearly to the thigh. The entire ensemble is in oxblood, with accents of gold and silver. She limns her face in similar colors: bronze and russet on the eyelids, a perfect slash of kohl, a radiance of rose-gold across her cheeks. For her mouth, the absolute red of a desert dusk.

"You're much more exciting to look at than I am," Nuawa says, fulfilling her part of the script, the kind of compliment she is expected to deliver. "A war god."

"You are dashing. The dress uniform becomes you."

That is, in its own way, as staged as Nuawa's. She imagines running her fingers along the texture of what lies between them. By now it would be as frictionless as satin, and as much a product of artifice.

They exit the apartment, Lussadh's tall heels clicking on the floor and their echoes racing ahead. The architecture is not always the same: there are lanterns resting on thorned plinths that Nuawa hasn't seen before. The palace is alive, as the general has said, and difficult to memorize. Nuawa has tried to explore, and more often than not finds herself lost. She can always return to their suite, but most paths outward are shut to her, as though the palace will permit her to see only so much. But when she is with the general, all walls and doors part like eager lovers, without sound or hesitation. They never see another soul when Lussadh doesn't want to be seen, even though the palace must be staffed and inhabited by hundreds.

Broad skylights from high above let in flashes of brilliance. White flowers crackle through the perfect black of Kemiraj sky, their petals jagged and their stems like whips. It has been a long time since Nuawa has seen frostworks. The last time she did, she was going into a kiln. She remembers now that she was limp, half-sedated. She touches her mouth. It must have been numb, bitter with the drug.

Lussadh leads the way into a wide corridor filling with the fresh-arrived crowd. At once the throng moves to give way to the city's lord. Nuawa follows Lussadh's wake into a tide of perfumes and zibeline silk, a hundred fluttering saris, scores of billowing hair-veils. Clockwork butterflies perch on necklaces and earlobes, wings fanning gently in rhythm to their wearer's breath. Jewelry snakes coil around wrists and forearms, thick lengths of silver and opals. Many of the guests opt for Yatpun brocades, though they keep the local predilection for paillette: a sleeve studded with pearl, a hem glinting with quartz.

The feast hall is larger than anywhere Nuawa has ever seen, larger than even the arenas in which she has fought and subdued leopards.

A herald speaks into their amplifier, "General Lussadh al-Kattan, Lord-Governor of Kemiraj, Commander-in-Chief of Winter!" They pause, either for breath or theatrical effect, before adding, "Lieutenant Nuawa Dasaret of Sirapirat, victor of the twenty-seventh tribute game, favored by the Winter Queen!"

The weight of attention that falls on her is sudden and comprehensive. Not even on the fighting floor was it like this, not even the tribute finale where she earned her hyacinth. Conversations cease and heads turn, and the silence that ensues is deafening.

Lussadh's hand brushes, gently, over her shoulder. Nuawa startles and draws a breath before she raises her chin, meeting the eyes on her with a short, sardonic bow and a sweep of her arm. Performance.

The pressure lets up after that, though she can tell there is more than curiosity in the gazes. They did not expect a Sirapirat at all, let alone a Sirapirat officer in her position. She is exotic, as she said to Lussadh, but in the way of exotic animals. An exhibit that has escaped its leash, and which must now be worked around or herded back into the cage. It is a new experience. Most of her life was spent in her native city, and she knows—as all do—that Sirapirat was the disgraced territory, black-marked for sedition. But in her work, it never mattered; her friends, managers, and contacts have all been Sirapirat. This open contempt, this disregard. Kemiraj is enemy territory for more reasons than its connection to the general.

She keeps a few paces behind Lussadh, the respectful distance of a bodyguard. This easily reduces her to an accessory and soon she is ignored while courtiers swarm Lussadh. Many of them are young women with scented, oiled hair and bright eyes and quick painted mouths. Like the rest, they wear heavy jewelry, clockwork pieces that whirr and drum and dance with tiny, pretty legs. Amidst them, Lussadh's clothes look ascetic. She lets the crowd lead her from food platter to food platter; she extends her wrist so a girl can perch a clockwork lizard on it, gives a low velvet laugh to someone's joke about the musician onstage plucking a qanun. By and by she settles in one of the many giant curtained birdcages that dot the hall, a fixture with a settee and a small table that quickly fills with plates of falafel, spiced olives, miniature ziva. The courtiers call for stronger drinks; more try to crowd into the cage.

Nuawa stays outside. By now the combined perfumes and colognes and hair-oils have grown as dense as smoke, and in any case Lussadh's suitors are liable to shove her out. So she stands by, watching fascinated as the general performs the part of the object. Something to covet, something to breathe in, her every utterance and exhalation waited upon. It is beauty that exerts this force of attraction, but more than that, it is power. The women that have alit on the general like moths believe that to breathe the air Lussadh breathes is to share in that, and to receive a touch from her fingertips—or the roundabout kiss of sipping from her wineglass—is a benison, a taste of possibility.

An older woman approaches. Even at a glance her importance is evident; she does not bother with the clockwork, the jewelry. Her hair is gathered in a long braid, sable and polished, but not so oiled that it runs the risk of dripping. Simple gold rings in her ears and a touch of bronze pigment on her eyelids and the center of her lips. She cants her head at Nuawa. "I'm Veshma, Minister of Commerce. By my reckoning, you aren't enjoying yourself. Is there anything I can do? Food more to your liking perhaps? I could have the musicians play something else."

Nuawa crosses her hands behind her back. "I'm here to guard the general."

Veshma puts her hand to her chest, in mock outrage. "You are not. You're here to be introduced to Kemiraj society, it's just that Kemiraj society consists of blind fools. Anyone with a functioning eye would've courted you as eagerly as they do the prince. That is, the general; pardon me. The clever ones would have pursued you with greater fervor than they pursue her, for you represent new opportunities, an unknown variable. Potentially you're much more available than General Lussadh."

She glances at the cage, meets Lussadh's eye briefly. The general gives an almost imperceptible nod. "I fear I would only disappoint. What have I to offer? I'm but a new lieutenant."

The minister clicks her tongue like a disapproving aunt. "You know exactly who and what you are. Captain Juhye was going to make your acquaintance, but he's held up by his own admirers." She gestures at a tall, spare man who wears the same dress uniform Nuawa does. He is surrounded by young men and has the expression of a trapped prey. "The palace can be an interesting place, if you have the disposition. Juhye doesn't. He is a soldier first and has come to his position by sheer hard work, not by playing games."

"And you, Minister?"

"I came to this post by tooth, nail, and blood." Veshma rubs at the back of her hand, finger lightly running over a thin bangle. She plucks a wine flute from a server's tray and offers it to Nuawa. "Some of the blood was not mine, but who is to quibble?"

Nuawa sniffs the wine and notes the acrimonious tint of a curse. She smiles and drinks regardless; the parasite will nullify whatever it is. "A sentiment many can sympathize with. Since you're the first at this party to treat me like a person, is there anything I can do for you, Minister?"

"No, no. It is what I can do for *you* that matters. Your impression of the palace should not be so poor. I must work hard to rectify it, by bringing you around to better company." The minister draws her toward the other side of the hall. "For a start, why don't we extract Juhye from that gaggle of nubile boys vying for his hand?"

"Assuming he wishes to be extracted. I am no judge of male beauty, but those appear comely enough." A selection of shapes and sizes: rotund or willowy, built like blades or hammers, faces long and gaunt or round and bright-cheeked. Whatever Juhye's tastes, there is one to suit.

"The captain is a private person and is already betrothed to a bride-to-be *and* a groom-to-be. I doubt he requires a third." Veshma advances, a vanguard in sari and anklets wading through the crush of young Kemiraj men. "Captain Juhye! Can we borrow you for a trice?"

He turns their way, looking immeasurably relieved as he excuses himself, smoothing down his battered sleeves without much success.

They look as if they've been yanked on by amorous hands one time too many.

The captain stops a few paces from Veshma and Nuawa. He staggers, one arm hitting the tray of a passing servant. A samovar crashes; cups scatter and dash, glittering, on the floor. Juhye falls to his knees.

Nuawa starts forward, then stays. If it is poison, perhaps the same she just ingested, there is nothing she can do. From the other end of the hall a palace chiurgeon is running and the general rising from her birdcage, shaking off her admirers. One of Juhye's darts toward him, crying out his name. Someone else shouts for help, and someone's child—dragged unwillingly along to the reception—tugs at their guardian's skirt and begins to whine.

Subsequent minutes dilate.

Human cognition imposes patterns, seeks the familiar in the strange. To Nuawa it seems as if an oneiric vision has spontaneously taken over her, and there is a burst of geometry where Captain Juhye should be. A tree made of glass has sprouted in his place, branches tipped in yellowed teeth, knife-edge leaves draped in guts. In the hyper-focus of this moment, she hears withheld breaths, shuffling feet, and the peculiar, distinct noise of flesh ripping from skeleton, a liberation of fat and ligament.

Then the smell. The steam of hemorrhage in the air, the stench of bladder and bowels letting go.

One of the guests howls, a raw animal sound, and falls. They erupt. A bright faceted explosion, as though an artwork has been honing itself inside human sheath all this time, biding for the perfect, exquisite birth. Vertebrae snap and give way to silicate; glass cracks and splinters under the stress of breaking free from cartilage and cranium. An uneven stalagmite stands where seconds ago there was a person clad in silk. Dewdrops of lymph and blood quiver on the milky crystal, oozing sluggishly down.

FIVE

WHEN ALL IS SAID and done, three people turned to glass at Veshma's party. Captain Juhye, a district judge, and a thaumaturge from the Ministry of Interior. Lussadh reviews the pertinent intelligence reports. They were all part of her own coup against Ihsayn; none were suspected of colluding with Sareha.

"Sareha's revenge from the grave." Lussadh turns over the metal kaleidoscope that holds a piece of what used to be Juhye. The fragment of glass revolves within the canister, suspended by charms of sealing and containment. The palace thaumaturge has found nothing in the remains. No trace of witching, no lingering grudge. It is just glass, as ordinary as any windowpane. "What do you think, Ulamat?"

"I'm thinking that I should have learned thaumaturgy, my lord." He rubs at the bridge of his nose. "I never did have any aptitude. But I would have been much more useful for you if I'd persevered."

"We have thaumaturges. None of them is any good at intelligence work. I'd rather have one of you than twenty of them." She folds her hands and leans back in the seat. They are in one of the boardrooms she uses for private audiences, the small necessary meetings that are free of pomp, sometimes conducted in the deep of night. As this is now. The feast is hours behind, the guests sent home pacified with reassurances that the Lord-Governor has everything in order. By morning the news will have spread like wildfire, whatever their efforts at rumor control. "Possibly a delayed curse, but the timing was perfect, wasn't it?" Juhye's teeth strewn on the immaculate floor, a few caught in table drapes, one swirling in a cup of chilled ouzo.

"The perpetrator must be at court still, yes." Ulamat takes a hearty gulp of his coffee. Black, steaming, entirely unsweetened. "There's the —well, we could find a scapegoat, but if it happens again ..."

"Yes, that is the problem, isn't it?" She is repeating him, repeating herself. "Whoever it is, they got us well and good."

"My lord?" He looks up at her, putting his mug down so quickly it clatters on the tabletop.

It is the first time, Lussadh realizes, he has ever heard her admit defeat. No matter what she has always had a solution, given small speeches. She has always *reassured*. Perhaps it is exhaustion. Perhaps it is the indelible sight of Juhye tearing and shredding, his mouth too wide, as he transmuted from skin to crystal. "You should get some sleep," she says. "You need it more than I do. I'll take another look at the scene of the crime."

"That cannot be safe."

"Our thaumaturges have checked and purified every centimeter of the hall. It's as safe as it can be." And she requires privacy to reach the queen. "Go, Ulamat. We will both think better when we have had a little rest."

"Yes, my lord. Before I leave—where might the lieutenant be?"

No point asking which lieutenant. "She has pressing matters to attend to, on my orders." With Guryin, but her aide doesn't necessarily need to know that. She means to be more careful with information from now on, even with her closest. As she should have been from the start.

She smooths her hands down the front of her dress. Sanguine matter has flecked it, though at a glance this merely blends into the oxblood fabric. It is a dress recently made by the queen's couturier, Her Majesty herself helping to pick the cutting, the colors, the style of seams. She was delighted to see Lussadh in colors like these, the deep red, the jewel tones. When Lussadh pointed out she hardly needed more clothes, the queen said, *Indulge me. It delights me to see you in beau-*

tiful things. The poets call you a work of art, but to me you're more like a confection.

Confectioners are artists, my queen.

To that the queen laughed before commissioning her more clothes. It is such a small thing, this memory, yet remembering it now is an ache. She misses her queen; she feels weak for the fact. The Winter Queen may never fault her for vulnerability, but Lussadh has stricter standards for herself.

Soldiers salute her in the corridors: there are more assigned than usual, double the guard detail, most of them infantry she brought with her from the capital since Sareha has all but emptied the local garrison. Guryin joked that it was a waste that Sareha didn't put them in the kilns—*So many bodies, and not a single ghost wrung out between the lot.* No doubt Sareha thought it another gesture of defiance to execute and cremate.

Lussadh listens to the echoes of her footfalls, the sharp clacks of heels on stone. Good shoes, built for stability and balance. She can easily stride in them, if not run, but they are loud. At the feast they adorned her well; now they only give away her position, announce her coming to anyone listening. And the perpetrator must be here somewhere, monitoring, triumphant. To have caused this much damage in so spectacular a fashion, at a moment when she was about to restore order to the palace and to the city at large.

In all her decades of service to winter she has never been struck at so effectively.

"Leave me," she says to the soldiers stationed inside the hall.

"All of us, General?"

"All of you. No one has disturbed the area or attempted entry?"

No one has. The hall has been under lock, key, and heavy guard: she counts twelve soldiers as they file out, one of them a thaumaturge. Once alone, she makes circuits around each glass sculpture. All three have been cordoned off, contained behind half-living vipers of obsidian and metal, substances that are conduits for warding. She tosses a fragment of smashed dinnerware over and one of the witched vipers instantly rears, snatching it out of the air. A crunching noise.

There is the bladed tree that used to be Juhye, twice as tall as he was, slender of trunk and branches. There are still organs trapped inside, like insects in amber, and spheres of congealed blood that never met the air: blue-black rather than red. The next is the stalagmite that used to be a judge. A length of entrails on the floor, one lung stuck within the crystal, several fingers knotted inside the pillar. The last, the ministry thaumaturge, is humanoid, bipedal. This one has retained the most body parts, the most fluids. An unblemished eyeball lolls embedded in the crook of a crystalline elbow, a piece of cartilage —ear or nose—abides in a narrow hip. A liver here, a kidney there, preserved in their entirety. Odd fleshy masses like tumors, and a solitary bezoar clotted in mucus and orange fur.

Lussadh touches her breast, the point at which her shard of glass resides. The parallel does not escape her—the glass within, erupting to horror without. Whoever is behind this almost certainly knows the secret of the queen's favored, of what winning the tribute tournament signifies and what Lussadh carries.

Her calling-glass is halfway out when she hears that sound of crackling ice. She follows the noise to the window, and there catches the familiar sight. A frost outline of a tall figure robed and crowned and brilliant in the moon.

She puts the calling-glass back, exhaling in relief. The queen has learned what happened, one way or another.

The frost sending leads her on, out from this floor, out of the palace. Strange that it doesn't simply bring her to a private, secret place in her wing, but the queen has her caprices. Lussadh exchanges salutes with patrols, her eye always on the ice figure that snaps and darts across the pavement. She does stop once to peer down at the city's lower tiers, at the commotion of crowds moving through night streets, freed at last from curfew, well-fed for the first time in a while. She watches a group of young people barrel out of a restaurant, laughing, bottles in one hand and shawarma in the other. Street vendors roast and distribute kebab, handing out skewers and small plates. What happened at the party hasn't reached them—for now.

She strides one level down to clerical offices and dormitories that house staff of limited means, limited ranks. Low, sloped buildings reinforced by crude iron. At the present they are vacant—their occupants either at the palace or down below, making the most of this single night.

The ice sending disappears outside one of the offices. She approaches, and at once knows Her Majesty is not here—not in person, not in envoy-casting. Lussadh's affinity does not stir, and her skin does not detect the shift that radiates from the queen, the drop in temperature, the change in air pressure.

Lussadh draws her gun. If she is mistaken, the queen will forgive.

On the ledge that overlooks the next level down, a person stands, hidden beneath a corpse's shroud. The white cloth billows, giving her features in fragments: broad wide-set eyes, nose like a needle, cheeks where skin is stretched tight over a skull as gaunt as a bird's.

This person is of Yatpun, like the queen. But Lussadh does not dwell too long on this thought. She shoots: a thunder of insect noise as frost-bees burst out of the muzzle—

And stop.

They hover about her in a nacreous cloud, thick, confused. They do not surge forward; they do not vent their hunger on human flesh as they've been made to. Between the shroud, the stranger smiles and unslings from their back a shark-sleek spear.

Lussadh does not allow surprise to slow her. She is ready when the first blow comes, catching it on her sword. Her wound throbs. The spear-tip slides along the length of her blade as she twists around and kicks at the stranger's midsection. Her heel connects with something that is more than flesh and muscle. Not armor—she knows how that feels and this is something else, not leather or metal mesh or even wood. Her opponent's breath hitches, yet they lose neither their balance nor impetus. The spear dips low to sweep her legs.

She leaps over it and comes down stamping on the spear, her weight pinning it by the haft to the ground. She swings, a sure, decisive strike.

The stranger lets go of the spear and pulls back, gaining distance. In their other hand a knife has appeared, as though out of thin air, long and the precise shade of black ice. Lussadh did graze them: a cut on their cheek has opened wide and deep enough that it exposes fat, a sliver of skull. But bloodless. Impossibly, it is bloodless.

They bend forward and charge her like a bull.

It is the wrong stance for a blade so short and Lussadh counters it with ease, chopping downward on the riposte. It should have severed their wrist but there is that again, the sense that her blade connected with a substance other than flesh and bone, the noise grating like metal on metal. She drives them back, away from the firmness of pavement, toward the creaking ledge. Their hand hangs, attached to their wrist by a slip of skin and white tendons. It should have immobilized them with agony. They fight on, parrying and fending her off with their good hand and one little knife even as they inexorably retreat.

In the next blow Lussadh puts her back into it, all her might. Her shoulder wound splits with a gush of warmth.

The stranger dodges, overcompensates, and loses their balance finally, the pavement under them wet and slippery with frost. Lussadh grabs their shroud and with that momentum heaves them over the railing. Panting she watches them plummet and dwindle into the distance below. She waits to hear the impact; it never comes.

Next to her, the fallen spear slowly thaws, melding with the snow into oily slush.

———

IN THE TEAHOUSE'S uncertain light, Nuawa can hardly recognize the major. If she was pressed she would not be able to express what precisely has changed—Guryin's features have not rearranged themselves the way Ytoba's did, and individually they may well have been the same as ever. This is not an act of shapeshifting, but some subtler practice that exerts not on Guryin's face but on the onlooker's perception, and it's not until xe grins and speaks that she is sure who xe is. "You look like you saw a ghost. Are you uncomfortable around thaumaturgy?"

"Not exactly." Nuawa has changed out of her dress uniform to plain clothes, though she keeps her weapons. The rendezvous point Guryin has chosen is a teahouse on the city's lowest level, the oldest part of Kemiraj. It is packed, drinks and food paid for by the palace's coffers. Both flow freely from what must be an overstressed kitchen. Every table bears a platter piled high with samosas and poppadum, bowls of chutney and paneer. "Something urgent happened at the palace."

"So I gather. Not to worry, I didn't invite you just to have terrifically greasy food—though this teahouse is rather nice, wouldn't you say, excellent ambience—but to give you a progress report. How was the party by the way?"

"Someone put a curse in my wine, but I imagine that's routine palace politics. Perhaps Minister Veshma didn't like the look of my nose." She keeps her tone casual: the minister is highly placed.

"Ah. Such is life among the lofty." Guryin points with xer chin. "Do you see that table by the window? Empty. It's reserved for an honored guest. Who eats for free, even on regular days. Always here for dinner."

"Yes?"

"Here ey comes. That person with the green hair? Ey's a chiurgeon of exceptional skill, specializes in flesh-molding. One of the best in Kemiraj, and Kemiraj is full of the best. What distinguishes em from the others is that ey does this—giving people the bodies they want—for a pittance."

Nuawa appraises the chiurgeon in question, a stocky person with dyed hair, dressed in a thick, loose kurta and trousers. Ey takes the seat. A waiter brings em fresh flatbread and full bowls of curry, better fare than any other table's, brimming with glistening mutton. "A philanthropist."

"And well-loved around these parts." Guryin pops a samosa into xer mouth and loudly slurps xer tea. "Ey's booked for a patient this night, after dinner. Ey's hurrying through eir food. You see?"

She cracks a poppadum in half. At the feast she ate next to nothing, and though she has no appetite now, she doubts she'll survive the night on an empty stomach. She swallows without tasting, chases it down with too-sweet lassi. To the back a table erupts in laughter and someone yells mildly obscene congratulations to a would-be bride. "And?"

"Your time at the Seven Spires was better spent than I anticipated.

Someone has petitioned our good chiurgeon for a total facial recon-
struction—I've made friends with eir secretary—and while the name
put down isn't Penjarej Manachakul, it *is* a Sirapirat name. What's
more, I sent word to Ulamat, he couldn't find the name anywhere in
immigration records for the last ten years or so. Safe to assume the
patient's living under an assumed name."

"This is all circumstantial."

Guryin makes another samosa disappear and gives her a sidelong
look. "Also, the best lead we've got so far."

And Kemiraj is a city of hundred-thousands; they must start somewhere. Nuawa concedes with a nod. They go through their platter,
Guryin taking the lion's share. Soon the chiurgeon finishes eir meal.
"We'll give em a head start," the major says in a low voice, dipping xer
fingers in a small washbasin the teahouse provides every table.

They vacate the teahouse. Their table fills up quickly: the night is
yet young, and few citizens want to head home yet after this long
cooped up in their domiciles.

Despite the circumstances, Guryin is casual, strolling along as
though xe is giving Nuawa a tour of this district. They lose sight of the
chiurgeon more than once, but xe always finds the chiurgeon again—
Nuawa becomes more and more certain the major's sight extends
beyond the physical. Once she looks for it, she spots out of the corner
of her eye a cobalt shadow that fleets across the dirty slush, an outline
of wings and beaks. In shape, a bird of prey. Not the sort that flies at
night.

The alleyways around them pull tight between old buildings that
slant toward each other like herd animals sheltering from a storm,
their brick walls made bright by graffiti layered one over another, their
awnings meeting to form tiny bridges and ledges on which birds and
laundry make their nests. Once this was where those of means lived,
Nuawa has been told, the entire district shaded from the sun by the
upper levels and overpasses. With winter, that has changed, and
wealth has climbed upward, to where it is warmest.

Past knots of public gardens where dark, faceless statues stand,
they come to what Guryin informs her is the district's hospital. A
square building, two storeys tall, with brutalist angles, shuttered

windows, and a corrugated gate. Busy even at this time of the night. The major makes a great show of sniffling and coughing to gain them entry, though a brown-uniformed nurse lets them know that—being non-urgent—they'll have to wait behind a long queue.

In a lobby crammed with patients—sprained ankles, fever, a few families here for their birth-chamber appointment—Guryin whispers to Nuawa that xe wants the chiurgeon to be in mid-operation before they interrupt it. "We want to catch your quarry red-handed, so to speak. And strapped down at an operating table, the nice professor won't be able to run. Let's see, we still have half an hour to go, so ... how did you meet *her*?"

"Whom?"

"The general, of course. I've been dying to know."

It hardly seems the time or the place. Nuawa surveys the lobby and the clusters of sick people. "We met in a library."

"Ah! I can see it now. You were poring over some complex, fabulously erudite manuscript, and that is what drew the general. She likes intelligent, intense people. I tried to introduce her to a bevy of those, but none struck the right chord, for whatever reason."

"The book I picked out was mostly pictures, actually. If I may—"

"So, the library. What next?"

She hardly has any idea, Nuawa realizes, where the chiurgeon's office or operating theater is. Whatever else, she has to rely on Guryin for that. She tries not to look at her watch. "She watched me fight. I assume she liked well enough what she saw. Beyond that I don't think it appropriate to discuss, with due respect."

Xe issues a *tsk*. "I don't mean the salacious minutiae. What do you take me for? Edit out the kissing, leave in the courting. Does she properly spoil you? If she does not, I'll tell her off."

"I really don't think—"

"Ah, you're right, we ought to get a move on. Have you ever been inside a birthing chamber? No? This way."

They blend in with prospective parents, moving to the birthing ward. A nurse passes them by, clad in layers of sanitation carapace, carrying an infant freshly extracted from a womb and damp with alimentary waters. Guryin turns to coo at twin babies carried between a trio of husbands, who beam at xer, proud. To Nuawa, xe adds, "Kemiraj subsidizes most of this, but even then, this hospital's ward is cheaper than most. Even the children of the enamel can afford it. This place has just three dozen wombs, so as you can imagine the waitlist is eternal."

"Do *you* want one of your own?"

"As a matter of fact, yes. My betrothed and I, we love children. We're thinking of two actually, but that'll have to be after the wedding —decency, yes? Imsou will want a grand reception. What about you?"

Nuawa strives to imagine the concept of wanting to raise children under service to winter; she cannot. At the door of another birthing chamber, a nurse speaks in a low voice to a young woman before presenting her with a small, swaddled corpse. "I can't say I have thought about it. I'm not the parental sort." Ytoba's scheme or not.

Guryin's eyes turn distant, glazed, as though xe is looking at a faraway vision—something relayed back by a familiar, perhaps. Xe flicks open xer watch and nods. "They've started the operation. The third door, down there, that's the one we want. Will you do the honors or shall I?"

Nuawa elects to: she is not, after all, the one working undercover. She marches forward and draws her gun. Nurses and assistants press in around her, blocking her way. "Lieutenant Nuawa Dasaret," she says, showing them her hyacinth. It gleams with a singular purity even under this light, a star nestled in her palm. "I'm here by order of Her Majesty. Absolute winter."

It is like thaumaturgy, after a fashion. They fall back like leaves shriveling in fire, whatever oath to healing they swore when they began their profession.

The operating chamber's door is unlocked. She enters, politely enough. Inside there is harsh, bright light: the chiurgeon wrapped in carapace and thick gloves, a slab of iron on which a person lies covered up to the neck, strapped in place and insensate.

"Doctor." Nuawa raises her gun and thinks of how she has become not just what she despises, but a thuggish caricature of it. Blunt force. Mindless action. "Your client is almost certainly a fugitive. I'm to apprehend her and would appreciate your cooperation. By all accounts, you're a citizen of sterling character."

The chiurgeon looks at her through the mask that leaves only eir eyes visible. When ey speaks eir voice is not entirely steady. "Officer— this is my patient. Can this ..." Ey takes a breath, loud. "Can this not wait?"

Nuawa thins her mouth and backs the chiurgeon into the wall. It helps that she is taller than em, more sturdily made. "Your patient. Has she ever gone by the name Penjarej Manachakul?"

Eir expression is hidden behind the carapace, but the flinching is answer enough.

Nuawa looks at the prone body, the face slack by sedation. Plain, with rounded eyes and a smattering of scars deepened by sun and age. A person who could have disappeared into any crowd. A gun makes its own dialogue; it is an instrument of brute monstrosity. She can conclude this now with a simple pressure—aim, trigger. The engineer would be dead, and the Winter Queen would be thwarted. But that would mean Nuawa's execution and leave much unresolved. The queen will not fall for lack of Penjarej.

She activates her calling-glass and contacts the nearest district patrol. "Corporal? This is Lieutenant Nuawa. I have a criminal suspected of treason against the Winter Queen. Yes, come at once. Absolute winter."

How odd to command the queen's personnel, and odder to be obeyed. It is borrowed authority, but it sits on her well, like a gorgeous pelt ripped from the furnace bodies of rare wolves. The words are simple, the act is simpler still. *By and by you shall become her creature in truth as well as pretense.*

SIX

THE PRISONER IS slow to wake, and Nuawa has brought a book to while away the wait. It is a slim volume with a garish cover, a tale of espionage and adventure in the occident. In these books, the western lands are feverish and savage, the women scantily clad, and no one has any manners. She turns a page to the part where the detective Sushmita infiltrates an occidental death cult where the faithful flagellate themselves with thorned whips and brand their feet with hot iron.

By the time the prisoner stirs, Nuawa is nearly done with the book: at this point the detective Sushmita has beheaded a wicked priest, liberated human sacrifices, and freed a few occidental women from their ludicrous corsets. Nuawa puts the volume away. On the cot her prisoner twitches and shudders as though in the grip of a nightmare and comes awake all at once with a rattling gasp. She watches Penjarej's expression turn from blankness to panic.

"It's not the best accommodation in the palace," Nuawa says, "but my colleagues would have stuck you inside a cell. This guest room is usually used by visiting dignitaries. Is it to your standards, Professor?"

Penjarej pushes herself upright, unsteadily. Her eyes fall on Nuawa, on Nuawa's uniform and hyacinth. Her breath leaves her in a rush, loud, as though she has been punched in the gut. "I—" She touches her face, groping for bandages and indentations, for rearranged cheek-bones and redrawn philtrum. Her hand drops. She goes quiet.

"There's water by your bedside. Do you need help with it?"

The woman reaches for the brass cup and takes hold of it with a shaking hand. She stares into it, at her reflection. Warped as it is in the cup, she must be able to tell that her face remains her own, the same one she was born with. She lowers the cup, brings it up again to sip. Her throat visibly undulates, as though the act of swallowing clean water causes strain.

Nuawa turns her chair around and straddles it—the only way to sit comfortably, this piece of furniture being mostly wire and a few twists of velvet. Whoever occupied this room before had strange tastes; the cot has a frame made of bone, reinforced by steel at joints and load-bearing points. Paper cranes dangle from the ceiling, swaying against scraps of scrimshaw and ivory. "Why do you think you are here, Professor?"

"I'm not—why would you call me that?"

"You work as a womb technician in the hospital. A long way from home and from tenure track at the Sirapirat Academy of Innovation and Applied Theory. Did your dean deny you equitable pay and make you resign?"

Penjarej rubs at her eyes and gets a good look at Nuawa, assessing her actual features rather than the symbol of the uniform. "You're the victor of the Sirapirat tribute. The first tribute to take place in Sirapi-rat." The engineer is already haggard, gray with exhaustion; she somehow blanches further. "I know who you are."

"Yes," Nuawa says blandly, "I too know who I am. I appreciate the thought, but I haven't spontaneously developed amnesia."

"You are—you're Tafari's and Indrahi's child."

She stares at Penjarej, all of her gone to stone.

The professor scrunches up a patch of blanket, her mouth pinched as though she wishes she could have unsaid it, could have swallowed back the words. She folds herself smaller still, pressing herself into the corner. "I don't plan to spread this around. I wish only to live as a subject to winter. Nothing else."

Nuawa counts in her head. One, two, three, four; whatever the roiling of her temper, that sequence does not change. "What were you," she says in a low voice, "to the women you believe were my mothers?"

"I was nothing. Just an acquaintance."

"That strikes me as tremendously unlikely." The more she speaks, the further she sinks herself into this trap. But she must know. She will secure Penjarej's silence, one way or another. "Among the queen's favored, I'm perhaps not the most charming. Would you rather speak to one of the others instead? General Lussadh is busy, but she could spare you a few hours." A bluff: that Nuawa cannot be blackmailed, that what Penjarej says—to the general, to anyone else—cannot possibly be used against Nuawa.

"No, I ..." Penjarej takes a deep breath. "I was more than an acquaintance. Yes. But that was in the past. I deserted their cause long ago. They merely consulted me—I helped them with some mechanical work here and there. Showed them the inner workings of a ghost-kiln as I understood it. I barely had any idea what they were about at first. Once I learned they were radicals, I left Sirapirat. Because I wanted nothing to do with that and because I was sure Indrahi would have me killed."

Nuawa is silent for a time, looking at this woman, this traitor. If what she has said is even true: Penjarej has nothing left to lose and would say whatever she thinks will secure survival. From her perspective, seeing the hyacinth, this confession is the safest path. Nuawa may well let her continue to believe that, for it is safest for Nuawa too. But Mother Indrahi would not have let so loose an end go, had she and Penjarej parted on terms as acrimonious as the professor insists. "What was that about then? The ghost-kiln?" Her voice is flat, even. An interrogator chasing potentially seditious information and nothing more.

"They had a hypothesis. That a body which goes into a kiln can survive it if it is in ownership of two souls, or at least two soul-like substances. And they were not wrong—the ghost-kiln is a simple machine, with finite capacity. I built them a miniature model, tested with pairs of mice sutured together. It was crude, but it worked and proved their theory more or less right. The mice didn't survive *whole*, but they survived."

"You can reproduce a ghost-kiln?" The secrets of whose making are privy only to the queen and a small handful of engineers. Kilns are made piecemeal, the parts transported and assembled in black-site ateliers. Nuawa herself has never witnessed the process.

"Not exactly. It was crude, approximate, it'd never have worked on people—only small animals, birds and rabbits and rodents. I have … an aptitude with certain types of machines."

The god-engine Vahatma. Nuawa wonders at this sudden overflow of information, this undammed willingness. And then at the planning her mothers did, down to this, to ensure that Nuawa would emerge from the kiln. Eight years old. She can hardly recall having been that helpless and that small. "All this is well and good, Professor. I'm pleased you have decided to be helpful." She laces her fingers together, leans so the seat tilts forward, precarious on its wire-and-velvet legs. "But Indrahi and Tafari Dasaret did not live under those names forty years ago."

Penjarej is entirely still, the way prey animals can be, as though they believe pretending paralysis can fool the predator into thinking them dead and therefore no longer interesting to chase. Even the professor's chest is held tight; perhaps she is willing her respiratory processes to suspend. A corpse gives up no information, cannot be tortured into answering questions.

"You clearly didn't sever ties as thoroughly as you claimed," Nuawa goes on, still in the same disinterested voice. "When did you last correspond?"

The professor blinks, hard. A tear. Two tears. They run and commingle. "Why are you doing this?"

"I don't know, Professor. Why are you?"

"Your mothers left you one last thing." Penjarej wipes at her face. "If you haven't already destroyed it. Tafari's diptych. There's a panel in the back, the only round one. Look for it and open it. Do at least that. You owe your mothers that."

Nuawa cocks her head. "You don't believe I would shoot you where you sit."

The professor turns to meet her eyes. "No. I do believe it. I do believe you would, without hesitation."

WHEN NUAWA IS ALLOWED into their shared suite again, she finds the general alone, looking deep in thought and more than a little wonderstruck. The gaze of someone who has been granted rapture, audience with a higher power, even if that audience didn't bring glad tidings. Lussadh nods at her, absently. "Pardon me. I didn't mean to lock you out of what is, after all, your room too."

"I heard that you were attacked, General." From Guryin, who told her not to take it personally that the general did not let her know right away. *She'll be talking to the queen first. It wasn't just any assassin.*

"So I was." Lussadh puts her calling-glass away and steps past the diptych. "Come walk with me. This concerns us all and I think better when I'm moving."

Nuawa does not allow her eyes to linger on the diptych. Time for that later—it is not going anywhere. Instead she takes note that this time there is no minimizing from the general, no waving the attack off as merely normal when one is on the field. Major Guryin has hinted as much, but this more than anything tells Nuawa the matter is grave, the assassination attempt out of the ordinary. She walks side by side with the general to the throne hall, Lussadh pausing on the way to tell the soldiers stationed there that she and Nuawa will have total privacy within.

Nuawa shuts the heavy door behind them. The general cranes her neck and shields her eyes from the skylight. Dawn has come prematurely and the first of it bleeds on the clouds, a dainty hemorrhage. "This was a much busier place once. There was so much memorabilia to dynasty and conquest. I used to think nothing about it could possibly change, but even the land is mutable, the cliffs and the crags, the mountains and sometimes the sea. Why not a throne and all that contains it?"

"I cannot say I've lived long enough to see landscape shift, General. You haven't changed out of your feasting clothes." She reaches over to a rucked sleeve, pulling it flat until it is again a smooth line. Her hand moves to the front of Lussadh's jacket where she repeats the motion, tug, pull. Her finger grazes bare skin. "Still looks good, of course, by virtue of who's wearing it."

"You're too gentle on my pride." Lussadh walks in slow circles around the dais. To the side are yet more of the faceless statues Nuawa saw in the streets, though these are clothed in pailletted sherwani, crowned in complex hairnets and bristling coronae. They don't look native to Kemiraj. "The man who attacked me is called the Heron. He was the queen's earliest retainer but deserted her ... a long time ago. She warned me—and I saw for myself—that he's exceptionally difficult to kill. The weapons Her Majesty grants us will not work on him. Most pertinent to you, he means to eliminate all glass-bearers."

"That is—why?"

"As to that, I am not privy." Lussadh stops and gazes, without seeing, at a tapestry stretched between two featureless figures: one holding a khanda inlaid with brass curlicues, the other holding a dismembered demon head with feline eyes and a tusked mouth. "Her Majesty did say that she lost a glass-bearer to him four decades back, before my time. The Heron ages glacially, but then so do some priests and alchemists. He can make ice into arms, and where winter reigns he's able to manipulate the frost somewhat. I'll start carrying conventional ammunition. The queen will come herself to handle him, though it'll be a while; she's presently preoccupied. She assured me that we are safe at the palace. The Heron has his tricks, but penetrating our defenses is beyond him."

Nuawa studies Lussadh's profile, the chiseled planes that give away no expression. "You seem shaken, General."

"Is that so?" Lussadh runs a hand down the demon head, down the neck where the sculptor—familiar with the details of a decapitation—made sure to add a drip of blood, a trail of spine. "The queen suspects what happened at the feast might be his work. The symbolism is too neat not to be, though she is certain the Heron is incapable of doing that specific thing to *us*. She did not disclose what might motivate him."

That lack of information—and perhaps by implication lack of trust from the queen—troubles Lussadh more than the encounter or the Heron's alleged powers. "Can it be envy? Of your place particularly."

"Possible, though the queen has never expressed interest in men." Lussadh turns to look at her, an eyebrow raised. "Glass-bearers all begin smitten with her. Some never stop, others wean from it, but without exception they are infatuated. Is that not the case for you?"

"She's magnificent in her grace and puissance, but I can't say the thought has crossed my mind." No more than the thought of bedding a cobra. "I felt a draw to you alone, albeit one I tried to put off."

"Oh? Why is that?" The tone light, teasing.

Lussadh is looking for a diversion: away from that vulnerability, that glimpse into the person underneath winter's general. Nuawa cants her head. This is an easy lead to follow; she needs only to respond the way leaves shift in the breeze or rivers flow to their natural courses. More than that, she wants. To be distracted from her own freight, her own weakness. She does not think of Penjarej— that gets in the way. "You seemed out of reach. No doubt you were used to receiving suit from marquesses and emperors." She hooks her hair behind her ear, making the gesture delicate, inviting. "While I *am* ambitious, the thought of bedding you was just too extravagant. Like scaling an impossibly high peak or hunting an impossibly rare tiger."

"And has it been a good, worthy hunt?"

"I've yet to come to a conclusion. You could persuade me."

"Indeed? I will have to outdo myself." Lussadh bends to kiss her hand and then draws her up to the dais. "The throne of Kemiraj is said to be indestructible. We are both strong; how'd you like to test that claim?"

The surface of the throne is etched in bas-relief, black suns with a thousand rays, an endless sky. No armrests in the way. Nuawa's breath quickens as Lussadh presses her into it, the stone cool against her skin, and removes her belt. Slowly the general winds it around her wrists, securing her to the throne. They've agreed on a terminating word that, once said by either of them, will put it all to a stop. She does not anticipate uttering it. Her belt is looser than she'd like, and she says, "Tighter, General."

The general chuckles and murmurs into her ear, "To think that I never imagined you'd be the type in want of tying up." The belt winds over a second time until there is no further slack, and though Nuawa could still break free, the illusion of restraint more than suffices.

She hears Lussadh move behind her. The general loosens her shirt; one hand slips under and plucks at her nipples. "A shame that I could prepare no other … paraphernalia. I might have blindfolded you."

Nuawa thinks of someone walking in on this, on her bound and panting, such a filthy and shameless sight. The idea turns her slick, slicker. "By your order, we will not be disturbed. What if they hear noises?"

"You're always quiet. I trust your discipline." The general's hands glide over her belly, dip low, then come up again to knead her breasts. None too gently, firm just as she likes it. A painted nail scrapes a line down her stomach.

When Lussadh finally pulls open her trousers, Nuawa turns her cheek to the cool stone, straining to remain silent. Lussadh is still clothed, not a single button undone, though there is a flush in her cheeks and her breathing is not even.

"I'm entertaining the idea of leaving you like this, wet and wanting. For a few minutes, or as long as an hour," Lussadh rasps. Two fingers become three; they make sopping noises inside Nuawa, incongruously loud. "Or I could keep doing this until you cry for mercy, and then I'd fuck you until you're insensate and that belt is the only thing keeping you upright."

Nuawa licks her lips. "I'd like to see you try."

Lussadh pushes her thumb into Nuawa's mouth, dragging it over her tongue. One of her hands has captured both of Nuawa's, holding them in place. It seems impossibly long before Lussadh slides into her.

The general is not small, and the angle makes passage excruciatingly snug. Nuawa clenches her jaw and braces against the stone, though pinned down as she is, there's little room for her to move. For a split second she pictures the Winter Queen in her place, yielding control entirely to Lussadh, and then the general bites her ear and it becomes difficult to think. In sight of Kemiraj's seat of power, *on* that seat, they push and strain, Lussadh keeping the pace a slow agony.

Eventually it is no longer possible to do so. The general moans into her hair, hips thrusting fast. Nuawa gasps and shudders and thinks, helplessly, that she will scream: so much for that self-control.

They collapse together into the throne and into the crumpled pile of their clothing. Nuawa kneels, her hands still tied, the general's seed warm on her thighs. "You're going to clean me up." She shifts her hips, inhaling at the brush of cool air on engorged nerves. Her shirt is halfway off, baring a shoulder, a breast.

"I shall be as attentive as any handmaiden." The general cups her exposed breast, lazily reaching over to loosen Nuawa's belt. "Your back will be scrubbed until it gleams, and your hair shall be oiled as though you were an archduke and I your humblest of servants. Why, should you wish, I'll lacquer your nails and perfume your throat, and warm your feet in attar."

Nuawa rubs at her wrist: it is imprinted vividly with belt buckle and sunrays. "We must do this again, General."

"Worth those marks?"

"I wouldn't trade them for the world."

SEVEN

NOON COMES QUICKLY. When Lussadh looks out the window it is to a city wall on which the sun has poured all its treasury, a largesse of endless gold. So different from in the queen's palace: there the light is wan, as if the queen herself has willed the sky and celestial bodies to her pastel tastes. Lussadh glances at Nuawa, who nestles in the furs, still asleep. It has been strange to settle into intimacy so easily, sleeping together naked, Nuawa's breasts against her back, their legs twined like braided ropes.

She watches the rise-fall of Nuawa's chest, the small but constant motion which signals that the body's alimentary processes turn in proper order. She kisses a pale, narrow shoulder that—like so much of Nuawa—is marked by thin scars. They hint at coherent shapes, like an augur's readings. She pulls the furs all the way up, tucking Nuawa in.

Lussadh puts on a fresh robe that smells of citronella. In Kemiraj everyone knows her preferences, down to the fragrance of laundry. Sometimes she likes to picture what this country will be like after her passing: who will govern it, in what manner. But it will not be her concern. She is no longer prince and succession no longer her task. The most she'd have to do is select a few candidates for the queen to appoint. None of the strife of choosing heirs.

Guryin is waiting in her office, holding a flat paper box in xer lap.

"Did you redecorate again, General? I swear this place never looks the same twice."

"It keeps things novel." She does redecorate every so often. Once this office belonged to one of her cousins, her fellow candidate to be king-in-waiting, and she has done what she can to remove traces of that cousin. Currently one wall is covered in masks: theatrical ones from Sirapirat, white horned ones from Yatpun, half-masks in the shape of hawks and monarch butterflies. "How's the prisoner Nuawa brought in?"

"Docile, though she wouldn't talk to anyone else but the lieutenant. She shakes and sweats like she's dying if I so much as pop in to take a look. I thought of leaving one of my shadows in her room, but in a place that small it's going to be … noticeable." The major waves xer hand. "Especially to the lieutenant, who seems awfully observant. And who is tricky to track—she blinks in and out of my scouts' sight. Very odd, since I never detected any charms on her, and I know she's no practitioner."

"Curious. She wasn't like that in Sirapirat." The court thaumaturge Lussadh brought with her to that tribute game had no issue scrying for Nuawa. Potentially a matter of being a glass-bearer, potentially something else. "What else?"

"Mm. She said in passing that someone witched her wine at the party—not as if she was concerned, so it's possible our lieutenant has protected herself against toxins. Her prime suspect is Minister Veshma, who picked out her glass. Interesting, don't you think?" Guryin turns the paper box over to her.

"As a matter of fact, it is. Keep an eye on the minister." Veshma survived both the coup and the feast. At any other time, she would not have thought the minister inclined to treachery, but in a time like this … Lussadh opens the box. The paper within, protected by lining, is on the verge of crumbling and so dark that the ink on it closes in on illegibility. She does not fault Guryin's craft—this is not xer specialty, and reconstituting ash into readable letter is no small task. "I didn't even know you could do this, and I've always thought you one of the best thaumaturges I know." Not in scale, for Guryin can manifest no miracles, but in finesse and application.

"You know me, General. All talent." Xe snaps xer fingers and a small shadow-hawk appears in xer palm. Another snap; it disperses. "To be sure, I was never this good before the queen granted me her gifts. Used to be I could maintain maybe a couple scouts at a time and none of them were this substantial. Don't let anyone know though, I like to look good in front of the other bearers."

That is news to Lussadh, though not surprising. The mirror increases and amplifies, often unpredictably. She gently handles the remade letter, spreading it over the glass of a lamp to better make out the words. Addressed to Sareha and written in Mehrut, in a hand she knows bears no resemblance to Nuawa's. There is nothing as convenient as a name, being signed merely *Your friend.* "Nothing conclusive." She returns the letter to Guryin: xe might be able to track its sender. "But this is masterful work. You must've long surpassed your old teachers."

"Only by the grace of Her Majesty," xe says primly. "My gut says Lieutenant Nuawa wasn't involved, and I'm not just saying that because she's nice to look at."

"You've been monitoring her. You may well know better than I do."

Guryin makes a *tsk.* "You've always rated your own judgment better than anyone else's, as is proper. Are you worried that she clouds it?"

Again, Lussadh imagines what it would be like to watch the breath stop in Nuawa, the last of it exhaled like the whisper of sand. Again, it is a difficult thought to bear, a spike of lightning in her throat, but it is not impossible: good enough. "No, but I believe in your intuition."

"My intuition is that if she moves against you, it would be something else—an act all her own, in solitude. The lieutenant views collaboration with contempt, by my reckoning." Xe daintily removes xer boot and props xer foot up on the divan. "Right now, I'd rather she isn't guilty. She makes you—not happy exactly. More content, maybe. Nicer to be around."

Lussadh pantomimes shock, putting her hand to her breast. "I should like to think I've never been such unpleasant company."

"You're excellent company, General, but these days you're more personable."

She smiles, as though she agrees, and perhaps she does. "The queen will come as soon as she can." Even now this country, the hottest part of the continent, quietly resists winter. Her Majesty rarely visits Kemiraj, and each time she does she must prepare for it, submerging herself in ghosts. Lussadh has borne witness to this, the queen drinking souls out of shot glasses and the sluggish plumes of them dying between her lips. It was medicinal—the queen did not enjoy the act, the taste. "We're well-defended here until then, as long as we keep to the palace. That includes you."

Xe grimaces. "So, we're to sit tight until she arrives and sorts this Heron out? I don't like that. There has never been a threat we couldn't meet. We are her swords, not mewling children she needs to protect."

"We have limitations. The queen has none. I know you were having fun out in the city and I hate to interrupt your fine time, but I'd rather you stay put unless you absolutely must."

Guryin mock-pouts. "Killjoy. Very well, I will remain here, cooped up in these beautiful rooms until I wilt from ennui. Maybe I'll debauch our icy lieutenant a little. *She* is in need of fun." Xe pauses. "General, you're turning a little red."

"I'm certainly not."

"Ah, I forgot." The major bats xer eyes. "You already visit upon her all the debauchery she could possibly require. Quantity *and* quality—"

"Enough of that or I'll tell Imsou on you." Lussadh touches her calling-glass; it twitches a drumbeat, one, two, three. "My aide is coming."

"Ulamat the Imminent." Xe laughs. "I'll stay, if you don't mind."

She does not, though when Ulamat lets himself into the office it is evident that he does. He does not let it show on his face—he's always had good control of his expression—but he gives Guryin a very correct salute: a sign that he accords someone the bare minimum and no more. "My lord," he begins and doesn't go further, waiting for her to dismiss the major.

"Report."

"Yes. The lieutenant has a cousin, the son of her aunt Indrahi Dasaret—a monk teaching at a theological college in Kavaphat, if you recall, lord? Indrahi's execution wasn't very public, but the son found out nonetheless." He pauses, knitting his fingers together. "A few days later the monk was found facedown in a lake. I have had his body retrieved; it's on the way here."

This she did not expect. "Why?"

"If we rule out the incident at the feast as the Heron's doing, then the lieutenant's innocence is surer. But her exoneration would be definitive with one final test. Indrahi Dasaret was a subversive and her son—"

"No." Lussadh pulls herself short. She has almost shouted. That is not like her, and it is nothing to do with how fond—or not—she is of Nuawa. "I will not test someone until they have a reason to hate me and move against me in truth. King Ihsayn liked to test people, Ulamat, in that very exact way, with that very exact result. Indrahi Dasaret is dead." By Nuawa's hand, after all. "Let that be. Corpses are corpses."

He flinches and now she remembers, when she took him in from the streets, how long it was before he stopped flinching from every-thing; how long it was before he stopped expecting to be beat for eating too much, for breathing too loudly, for not learning his letters instantly. "I beg your pardon, my lord. I am unwise." He lowers his head, falls to his knees.

"You meant well." She takes a long breath; the king used to closely observe how she and her cousins carried themselves, and that extended to how they genuflected—dropping too fast, not enough poise, too arrogant. They were not punished, not exactly, but the king's disapproval would be known, and it would sit under the skin like a trapped thorn. "On your feet. Be at peace, Ulamat. Just have the body sent elsewhere, have it dealt with the respect a monk deserves."

———

ONCE NUAWA IS certain the general has left the suite, she shakes the sheets and the furs off. She is alone, naked save for the bandages on her wrists, still damp where Lussadh rubbed ointment into them. Her feet likewise oiled and wrapped, for the general fulfilled her promise to warm it in attar. *The arch of your foot,* Lussadh said as she stroked it, down and up. *How perfect it is, like the rise of a dune. The catenary of your hips, the way your skin runs, it feels as if I could lick a sky out of you.*

She doesn't bother to put clothes on. In the parlor she listens for the telltale signs of a familiar. In small enclosed spaces, they are not impossible to detect if one knows what to look for: a warping of light or a bending of shadow, a thrum in the air like thunder's consequence. Nothing. She is alone.

The diptych is veiled by a riot of bronze ferns and blooming chain cacti so bright they look as painted as the sky that Tafari put onto canvas however many decades ago. She circles the frame, running her fingers around the brass tracery that rims the diptych, avoiding the canvas or paint itself. Her throat closes and she wipes at her eyes, taking a deep breath. To weep before this, an ensemble of wood and metal and canvas. How grief's fault lines make a child of her, how they make dross of intellect.

She thinks back to that precise moment in the kiln, where she swallowed that cold, sharp thing. When she opens her eyes again, all of her is honed to a single point, a purpose as calm as a grave.

As Penjarej said, there is a panel in the back, a lone disc among trapezoids and rectangles. It detaches surprisingly easily, a simple brass plate, not much breadth or dimension to it. She presses it to her pulse-points one by one. She turns it about, holds it close to a ghost-pipe, and tries breathing on it: all to no result. Blood, or else—she locates her sliver-knife, a weapon of needle slimness and piscine ribs. She slices off a piece of her own shadow. The etheric pain is immediate, striking marrow-deep. She grits her teeth and catches that sliver of her spirit. To the touch it is wet, like living tissue.

She brushes it across the disc. The metal splits neatly in half.

Inside, a small cube of dark celadon, so smooth and richly colored it could've just cooled yesterday. It rattles when she moves it, little clicks against the worked earth: bone fragments or molars or gritty ash. Tafari's. The other object is a folded paper, good thick paper that must have been witched, like the painting itself, to withstand time and damage. The texture of it is crisp, and the ink on it the clear, direct green of malachite. She spreads the paper out. The letter is in cipher, one of the many Indrahi taught her almost as soon as she understood her letters. Shift the abugida this many places forward, the vowels this many places backward. Literacy in code, Indrahi used to say, is as important as any other. Acquiring it is much like acquiring a second language, and as fundamental to a good education.

Nuawa translates as she reads.

One to wake. Two to bind. These are the laws that govern those of the glass.

Our daughter, when you came into the world, we dreamed of victory. So close were we to the cusp that we thought we would raise you in a world of monsoons and warm rice, mangoes and all the sweet things that we'd regain once the Winter Queen had been repelled.

Tafari was a field chiurgeon in her time, and when we found him, he was deeply wounded, a shard of glass in his throat like dying. Nevertheless, he could speak as though his trachea had not been pierced, and he told us to take this glass right out, without breaking it. Not that we could have.

It was in a shadowed, stinking alley. Tafari and I had just conceived you, and I bore you within me waiting for the months to turn and you to grow large enough to be transplanted into an iron womb. Between us there was new life, and a future that we imagined as luminous as a summer day. In this alley he gave us a promise; without that we might never have granted him aid.

I am a servant of the Winter Queen and I have deserted her side.

There was no way to corroborate his claims, save the evidence of his own body. There was no blood, never any blood. The shard left him open and beneath the skin there were translucent structures crisscrossing the muscles; capillaries of the same material wound around his bones and drew cobwebs over his organs. He let Tafari dissect him to prove his good faith and his story.

He called himself the Heron; no other name did he give us. Perhaps it is a custom in Yatpun for those who worship the god Kidashoten, or perhaps it is particular to him and the queen he betrayed. Why he left her we never learned, for that alone he kept close to his chest. But much else he confided in us, the secrets that he asserted belonged to the queen.

This, then.

As the Heron has it, the queen was once a snow-woman created by the mountain gods of Yatpun. Her kind was made to be weapons, in a war that he insisted neither you nor I could possibly comprehend. Most of her sisters did not have what we might call volition. The queen developed hers by accident and came to resent her place, the place of a tool, hungering for more: to see what else she could do with herself, to see the earth beyond Yatpun. What happened next, you can surmise. She stole a mountain-god's treasure, a mirror of vast puissance, a mirror that is also a gateway. She studied it, she listened to its song, and in time she gained mastery over it.

Through this mirror, she stepped into our world, taking with her the first of her votaries, now her fellow exile.

(Are you human, we asked him. *Yes, I was, at the beginning.*)

Her mirror did not bear the stress of her passage, and on the shore of our world—on our side of Yatpun's event horizon—it shattered in her lap. But it was not only a mirror, and what it became was not only glass. Each of the shard was a seed, and in suitable soil it would gestate, mature into fruit. The Heron was the first, and through him she discovered that the shard fed on the human heart, granting its host marvelous strength. A bearer of this glass doubles the breadth of their soul and their self, and that is no small thing.

Yet the Heron did not suffice. To ensure success she scattered her mirror far and wide, letting it seek suitable hearts, letting them ripen for the harvest. The Winter Queen's desire is at once simple and unthinkable. She wishes to return to Yatpun clad in glory, in her full might; the mirror restored will allow her to pierce Yatpun's shield. There she will conquer, adding her birthland to her dominion, making of the mountain-gods either her slaves or vassals.

The mirror shard fostered in the Heron's body is the same that resides now in yours, a fruit half-grown. It would not grow within Tafari or myself, because we were adults. It would not grow in your brother, who was by this time too old. It required a young child. Yet we could not sacrifice you on a fable. There was no proof. There was only a shard of glass, steel-strong and brilliant, yet merely glass.

Years after the Heron left us, a link in our hidden chain snapped, and delivered you and Tafari to the kiln for crimes of sedition. And what could have saved you inside the kiln if not the fable, the shard as a decoy soul that would be harvested in place of yours? When I collected you, I thought it impossible, but the Heron's claims—in that at least—proved true.

The mirror shard will, or already has, made you potent and to the queen irreplaceable. She will come for you and hold you close. To her, you will be the greatest of prizes. She will kiss you, the first to wake the shard, though yours will already be woken. She will kiss you again to bind you to her, though the Heron asserted you will remain free.

This kiss symbolizes transference, an exchange; each time she touches the mirror shard inside you, she becomes—for a single instant —that close to flesh and marrow, that close to us. The substance of her softens. Her heart becomes arterial. She will be vulnerable to blade and ballistics.

My child, we forged you as a weapon. This you already knew. But not the extent of it, the breadth of what we've done, the decision we made on Tafari's sacrifice in the ghost-kiln. The sacrifice that we now, at the last, must ask of you.

But this is not what we meant to do, not at the start. Believe this, if nothing else. We saw ourselves bringing you up in the Sirapirat we knew as children, a Sirapirat where you will not have to guard yourselves always against the killing cold. A gentle world, a good world. We had thought the Heron would give us the secret to her defeat. And he did—but not in a way we thought. We believed it would be difficult, immediate, bloody. We believed it would be tomorrow, not in decades.

I did not think I would have to watch Tafari walk into the kiln. I did not think I would have to watch you enter it with her, hand in hand. No wife or mother should have to. Two species of creatures commit unthinkable atrocities: the tyrant, and those who fight them.

The rest, our daughter, is yours to decide.

EIGHT

WHEN GURYIN DRAGS NUAWA to the other side of the palace, to the disused wing where the dead king resided, she expects to meet someone or something grander than a jeweler. "Lieutenant Nuawa wants to commission a piece from you," xe is saying. "Isn't that right, Lieutenant?"

She looks from the major to the squat, thick-handed man Guryin has brought. He doesn't look like much, dressed plainly, but artisans who work with expensive materials tend not to wear their own pieces. "Do you work with flowers, by any chance?" She considers the jewelry Lussadh wears. Nothing on her fingers or wrists. "A pendant, I'm thinking, shaped like an anthurium."

He notes down her preferences for metal and stones—she declines the latter and asks for plain metal—and guarantees that it will be finished within a few days. Nuawa pays half upfront, not that the jeweler dares to ask for any.

"You *do* remember what I told you about Lussadh's favorite flower," Guryin exclaims once the jeweler has been escorted to the palace exit.

"I have a fair memory and you are right that I should get something for the general." Even if it must be trivial compared to anything else Lussadh owns. "But the real reason you called me here?"

The major shakes xer head. "So suspicious. This is a good spot for people-watching, when there are people in need of discretion and stealth. Look out this window. It's nice and small, and from the outside—down in the garden, say—it's almost invisible."

Nuawa looks and, indeed, Minister Veshma is emerging into the garden. In this section of the palace, garden means stained fountains and bare stones: no one has maintained it, and nothing grows here except for a dune chameleon, a lizard the size of hunting hounds, dozing in a corner. Veshma paces the area, head cocked as though listening for something. Whatever it is does not please her; her expression contorts. She throws down her fan, a tortoiseshell ornament that looks foreign, and scurries indoor.

"Odd," Nuawa concedes, "but it doesn't look conclusive."

"She's been here every other day. Nobody ever shows up and she doesn't do anything so obvious as pick up a secret letter or similar. I got my hand on the bangle she wore to the party, and there's nothing on or in it except this *tiny* whiff, sour, like a recently faded hex. It's a shame really—she gave herself away trying to poison you. Why would she make such a reckless move?"

"She must have especially hated the look of my nose."

Guryin snorts. "She's close to the general—well, used to be, at any rate. Part of the old guard Lussadh recruited for her, ah, historical event. Do you want to bring this to her?"

"The general will take it better coming from you." And it ought to keep Guryin occupied for the next hour or so. Nuawa has her own errand to attend.

———

PENJAREJ FREEZES, mid-pacing, when Nuawa enters. The professor looks caught, red-handed at a forbidden activity, as though she thinks she ought to remain as bound to the bed as a shackled dog, fetal and whimpering.

"What you said and what I read in the letter don't line up," Nuawa says without preamble, once she is sure there's just the two of them.

The room is windowless, and there is no sign of Guryin's etheric scouts. "One or the other must, of necessity, be false."

Penjarej keeps to her side of the room, as far from Nuawa as possible. She has moved the cadaverous furniture around, arranged it into a crude barricade coyly draped in tattered silk. "Have you made a decision, Lieutenant?"

"I'm curious as to your testimony. You implied the Dasarets intended to enter the kiln." And on purpose sacrifice Tafari, sacrifice Nuawa. To forge her better, faster, turn her into a weapon that simple training could not produce. "The letter suggests otherwise."

"My memory is not what it used to be."

What were her mothers like, Nuawa wants to ask, in those days before history exerted its weight; before they began building a future that she would come to inherit. How they had met, was there a sedate courtship or a stunning whirlwind romance. The things a daughter would desire to know, those pieces of the past that should matter more than anything. "Nor does the chronology align. Your acquaintance with them must have been concurrent with ... a great deal of pivotal events. I'd judge that you were there all the way up until Tafari's execution. Perjury before a representative of the queen—me—isn't something you want on your record, Professor."

Penjarej's fingers convulse. "How did Indrahi die?"

Like an open wound. Nuawa can almost taste it, the sudden rage, the wish to see this woman cast off a high balcony and shattered on the cobblestones. Her mothers died; this woman lives. Instead she smiles, calmly. "I executed Indrahi Dasaret myself, as is right and proper, for I serve as one of Her Majesty's swords."

Penjarej starts crying and Nuawa almost does it, pull the trigger and shoot a round into the wall next to Penjarej's head. This display of tears and mucus, these unearned theatrics. But the professor stops almost as abruptly as she started. She rubs her sleeve across her face like a child. "She loved you. They both did. They bought this iron womb and they nursed it in their house, counting the days, watching you grow inside. They'd tell me how many months or weeks were left, they got baby clothes and asked me which milk was best for infants, as if I knew anything about milk. They couldn't talk of anything else. You were the world. They wanted to meet you so much, they wanted to give you everything, they couldn't bear to put the glass in you. They delayed and delayed. Until Tafari was arrested and there was no longer any other choice."

"How tidy," Nuawa says and watches the professor try to regain the breath she expended in that deluge of words. "Of their collaborators and contacts, who else is alive?"

"Nobody." Penjarej stares down at the floor, her shoulders sagged and her arms limp.

Nuawa says nothing, moves nowhere. She waits Penjarej out. But the older woman stays quiet too, perhaps hoping that Nuawa will forget that she exists and go away. Conversationally, Nuawa says, "A foreign demon tried to lure me to act against the queen, to bait me into treason. Ey made marvelous promises."

"They were empty."

"While you make none at all?" Nuawa lets her words congeal, like poison inside a slice of persimmon. She wonders if Penjarej knows about that too, the fruit tree in the glasshouse, nurtured for lethality. Just as Indrahi nurtured Nuawa, to much the same result. Her mother plotting for death from the beginning, perhaps from the day of Tafari's dissolution within the kiln. A child, a persimmon. "Why do you do anything, Professor? What do you want? Winter may not be the ideal state of the world, but there has been worse. I know my textbooks, and Sirapirat was ruled by warlords back in the day. The world turns on an axis of butchery. Different butchers, that is all."

Penjarej shuts her eyes. Blocking out the sight of Nuawa, the lines of resemblance that must run down to her from Indrahi and Tafari. The point of the nose, the slant of cheekbones, the crook of the mouth. "You wouldn't understand."

"I suppose plenty of people devote themselves to things they can't see or have never seen, like the goodness of human hearts or what lies within stars. What might a restored Sirapirat look like? You and I don't have the faintest idea. Who or what might replace the Winter Queen? You haven't thought about that, either." This is as far as she can push Penjarej, Nuawa judges. She raps her knuckles against the nearest table—Penjarej startles, her eyes snapping open—and makes a show of listening for something. "Ah, now we're alone. How did you like it, Professor? Was I convincing?"

"What?" The single word is a whistle of air through teeth.

Nuawa tosses her head a little, smiles, affecting warmth though she is well-aware she lacks the disposition. "We were under surveillance, as a matter of course. But it appears I've intimidated and tormented you enough that my colleague is satisfied nothing untoward will happen in this room. I'll tell you why you are here—it's nothing to do with your past. The queen has little interest in history; if anything, she finds it dull."

"What?" Penjarej says, softer this time.

"She wants you here for the same reason that Kemiraj assassin went to you. I will tell her that I have persuaded you to work for her, and she will bring here the pieces of the god-engine Vahatma. This is something she badly desires, and the Winter Queen does not covet without reason." She takes the diptych panel out of her jacket and holds it out to Penjarej. "Together we could discover her true goal and bring about her fall. What will you decide, Professor?"

———

LEAVING BEHIND PENJAREJ'S CELL, Nuawa sights down Ulamat standing beneath a chandelier of moth-bulbs that give off a lacey, shivering radiance. Too far from Penjarej's room for him to have eavesdropped. Nevertheless, he looks furtive.

"Lieutenant." He curtsies.

"Does the general require me?"

"Not exactly, sir. There's just something you will want to see, if you have the time? I've had it delivered to one of the courtyard sheds. It took some doing—we had to put districts on lockdown again, what with the hysteria, stories about the party spread around and grown wild. Still, mostly under control. The city has faith in my lord."

They exit to the courtyard where prisoners have been brought out, plucked from Veshma's guest list. Nuawa counts six, though she is unable to tell who they are or what rank they held, what criteria were used to determine their proximity to Magistrate Sareha and therefore to guilt. They have been stripped down to underclothes—a thin choli, a gauzy wrap, a lungi. None is adequate to the weather. On the frigid flagstones they kneel and tremble, their exhalation steaming in the cold, their teeth chattering: Nuawa can hear it from where she stands. A soldier walks circuits around the prisoners, slapping their palm with the hilt of a baton, staccato and loud, a presage of the near and immediate future. Hard wood, pliant flesh.

Barring a couple, none of the prisoners are military. They are older, in their sixties to seventies, and soft. They must have just been brought out from a ghost-heated room or carriage—there's still vapor on spectacles, and icicles have rapidly formed in their hair.

Nuawa stops to watch. A light flurry begins to fall. The mind etches strange grooves and pathways into itself, for Nuawa thinks not of this courtyard but of the time she went into the kiln, her giving-mother with her. Her recall before that point has nearly been extinguished. To her understanding most people retain a better grasp of their life at eight or seven than she does. Hers is a canvas entombed by snow.

The soldier goes by each official, forcing their chin up with the baton's tip. The same questions rattle off: *For how long did you know of Magistrate Sareha's treachery? You were appointed to your post by her, how is it possible you claim ignorance? Do you know what it means to defy the Winter Queen?* Sometimes for variation the soldier would ask the prisoners how long they believe a human body can last under this temperature, from now until midnight; whether they expect to see the dawn. An ash-gray man loses control of his bladder. Piss soaks down his kurta, splattering onto the soldier's boots.

How does it feel, she muses, for these people to have been complacent all their lives, assured that they're favored by Lussadh and therefore guaranteed an easy life under winter? How it feels, now.

"I see we'll soon resolve the issue of Sareha's co-conspirators," she murmurs as she follows Ulamat into the shed.

"Some of it is to settle old scores. Those officials were never the most competent or the most loyal, and this was an efficient way to get rid of suboptimal elements."

Not so guaranteed after all. She looks around the shed as Ulamat turns on the light. A shelf of watering cans and pruning shears, a rack of shovels and rakes. It is a far humbler arrangement than she expects of the palace, but then there must be places for the mundane work, the menial labor that underpins the posturing of power and governance. She muses whether she could ask to see the kitchen.

Ulamat fiddles with one of the cabinets. "Here we are," he says, dragging into view a casket.

It is out of place in this shed, made of camphor wood worked over with golden curlicues. The sides are emblazoned with the banners of radiance, verses for passing and reincarnating. A saffron cloth covers the casket's lid, signifying that the body within belongs to a monk. Nuawa stares at it, confounded at what this might—

The aide lifts the saffron cloth and unseals the casket. Inside is a monk in his late forties, well-fed and up until recently healthy. He has been expertly touched over with wax and pigment, but there's no hiding the bloating that happens to flesh left too long in the water: he died by drowning. In the hachure of his features, the same cartography as her own is written—the reflections of Tafari and Indrahi. He and she, the two remaining images that show the world that their mothers ever existed.

Now there is only her.

The mirror shard inside her numbs who she is, what she feels. It leeches her humanity, perhaps converts it to something else, and that thought must have summoned something—the hallucination, the inexplicable phenomenon. The shed dims, the casket and Ulamat recede, and she becomes the single source of illumination. Her skin like a veil, and the tendons underneath overrun with crystals.

But as before, this vision disperses. There's just the corpse and Ulamat and her. "I recognize him," she says in a voice as impersonal as a mortician's. "My aunt's son. We were not close. By the time he left to ordain, I wasn't even in puberty. His departure allotted Aunt Indrahi more funds to spend on my keep and education, for which I am grateful. Am I to do something about this as his next of kin?"

Ulamat's eyes dart to meet hers, as if even *he* is alarmed by her lack of reaction. "Indeed, Lieutenant. You would know the proper rites."

"I will send this to the Seven Spires' scriptorium, the bhikkuni there should see to the matter properly. Send her an offering in coin and food. Luang-mae Kabilsingh should appreciate a few sacks of rice and spices, and fruits if we have any to spare." Nuawa straightens. "I mean you no insult, but this is a waste of my time and yours. My cousin—though I cannot claim him as that, as he renounced all worldly ties at twelve—would have been taken care of in Kavaphat by his temple."

"I'm admonished, sir. I will deal with the matter as you've instructed." He bows.

"See to that," Nuawa says. The air is too close, the shed too small. Dust and rust and decay. "I'm going to get some fresh air."

Away from him she draws a lungful of cold. The body has a capacity; it stands to reason that if she fills herself with morning crispness, it will displace the rest—sentiment, anger—and seal up the soft places where she can be hurt. She has not thought about him for a long time, the brother who was too old for the mirror shard and who therefore did not have to bear her fate. The brother whose name she is already working to forget. Why is he dead, she could have asked, demanded it from the general's aide, when he lived in the most sheltered place in the world, when he had forsaken Mother Indrahi and her history. The cause of demise wouldn't have mattered. As she studied the corpse with forensic detachment, she could only think of what she might do to Ulamat.

And Lussadh could not possibly have been ignorant. The general does not miss such things.

She walks faster, long military strides, through the garden and past the palace gates: none stands in her way. She walks without thinking, peripherally aware that she is beyond the reach of the palace's defenses, the unseen veils and bulwarks that keep them safe from the Heron. But it does not occur to her to care: what she needs is distance, what she needs is solitude. Given a few hours she will recover, she will regain her equilibrium and her ease of dissembling. She will continue on as she ever has, plucking at the strings of history Penjarej shares with her, returning to the silks and opulence of Lussadh's bed as if nothing has changed.

Someone is calling her name. She does not stop. Her march is long, and she intends to complete it, even if that means circumnavigating every level of Kemiraj. To keep her heart pumping, her muscles pulling, until exhaustion overtakes her and blanks out all thoughts. Behind her footfalls pound the pavement, the noise of pursuit. Nuawa quickens her pace, turns in to a narrow street hemmed by stone tenements and angular lampposts, and statues with the starved limbs and narrow fontanelles of marionettes. The path is a dead end, terminating at a sheer pitted wall, above which a tree peeks—bent under its own weight, dense with leaves the color of lampreys and fruits like lidless eyes.

She looks over her shoulder, by necessity. The general has caught up with her, must have run as fast as a demon of the storms. Lussadh is not even winded, though her brow is alloyed with sweat, electrum-bright. Nuawa thinks of what she will say next, what she will do, as she stands there facing Lussadh.

The general's eyes widen. She begins to move, and perhaps in a different time—when she has not already spent her breath on the run —she might have sidestepped it. Nuawa hears the whistle of momentum, sees the glitter of black ice.

The spear goes through Lussadh, its trajectory perfect and smooth. Lussadh staggers backward. When she tries to breathe, a wet rattle results.

Nuawa whips around. The Heron—that is who he must be— stands atop the high wall. White all over, whiter than even the queen: chalk, powdered pearl, new paper. Wings fan across his back, pinions cascading over naked hips and armoring his flanks, an image of the queen's god Kidashoten. A tuft of eider on his breast, plumage on his head in place of hair.

His stance is faultless, and in his hand a second spear builds, sleek and bathyal-dark. It is a beautiful weapon, despite everything, and it could have been made by a weaponsmith with intimate knowledge in the habits of weaponry—balance, wind resistance, penetration. She can see white hairlines along its shaft, even from this distance. Nuawa starts running, and as the spear shears through the air she shoots at its shadow.

The spear falls, its velocity wrung out, and shatters on the ground.

Nuawa heaves herself onto a window ledge, then a balcony. Up she climbs until she gains the roof, above the Heron. She sights him down, takes aim. He regards her with dark eyes fringed in pale, tiny coverts. The small wings at his side unfurl and catch her bullet. She keeps shooting; those wings keep intercepting her fire.

On the roof tiles her sword's shadows have spread a thicket of long hooks and bristling spines. She holds the blade out, its echoes rippling around her. "I'm the child of Indrahi," she says, first in Ughali then in Mehrut.

He gives her a long, curious look but says nothing. He produces yet another spear and advances, leaping up to the roof with avian ease. This close, Nuawa can see that the same silvery lines that reticulate his spear run over his limbs.

She keeps as far from the spear as possible, letting the shadows do their work. Each time they overlap with the Heron's they shred his wings, feather by feather. When she is forced to meet his blows, she lets them glance off rather than try to contest their strength. It is a narrow battlefield they have, but that is to her advantage—the echoes of her blade run wide, impossible to avoid. "The mirror shard you left in *Sirapirat*," she shouts.

He gives no sign of hearing her or even understanding human speech. His wings fray and his feathers fall. She strikes his spear hard enough to break and still it does not give. She carves lacerations into his flesh and still he does not slow. His expression remains vague, lazy, and he holds his ground.

In the world, as far as Nuawa is concerned there are three of them: the general lying broken below, Nuawa herself, this creature the Heron. And then, as though time has distended, there are four.

The Winter Queen stands manifest, shining with a hard, mentho-lated light: the pits of her eyes are black starbursts. She grabs the Heron by the back of his neck, lifting him up as though he is airy floss and desiccated leaves. There is a crack, a snap, of breaking bones. She flings him off the roof, down into the black, wet tree with its golden fruits.

In her other arm she has hold of General Lussadh, whom she

cradles without effort. "Come with me," the queen says. "She is prone to mortality, after all this time, and I can only delay its onset."

Nuawa does not ask. She takes the queen's hand. Her teeth rattle, her sight turns to gauze and harsh brilliance. In a moment, they are elsewhere.

NINE

THE CHIURGEON HAS FORBIDDEN Nuawa entry—she is a potential contaminant, and they are operating on a very open wound—but they have not forbidden the queen. Nuawa is left outside the sickroom alone, and she uses that time to contemplate her own condition. She has not bothered to clean and there is dried blood on her sleeve. Lussadh's blood, by process of elimination: she has not lost even one drop and the Heron does not bleed.

It has been, perhaps, an hour.

When Guryin sits down beside her, she blinks slowly at the major. Then she realizes xe has been there for some time, and her awareness has somehow elided xer. "Major," she says. "Her Majesty's with the general." Which Guryin must already know. She is being redundant.

"You're in shock."

Her hands are shaking. She stares at them, at the fingers trembling as though they've been seized by palsy, an abrupt acceleration of age. "I am?"

Guryin takes hold of her hands. Frowns. "Icy. Yes, you are. That's normal. If Imsou'd been struck down, I would be a wreck too. Happens when you're in love. Don't think less of yourself for it."

"I'm not—I don't think ..." For the instant, just as the spear struck, she hated the general. "That is an inexact way to put it, Major."

"Ah, you're one of those people. The ones who don't want to admit it in so many words. Stoic and intense is a *magnetic* combination, absolutely, but you don't have to keep it up every waking minute. It doesn't make you weak, just honest. I hope you will get around to telling her that you love her dearly."

She gathers herself, as best she can. Her hands continue to twitch; she clenches them tight. "You seem very certain that the general will pull through."

Xe draws xer knees up, cants xer head toward the tight-shut door. "I'm worried, very worried. But. The queen is in there, overseeing the process. Or breathing down the chiurgeon's neck, at any rate. The queen is not luck or prayer or even fortuity, my friend. She is the deific force itself. What she wills, she causes to transpire. She wants our commander alive, thus Lussadh *will* live."

"You put an extraordinary amount of faith in her."

"I've seen what she can do. So have you. She doesn't do much saving of life and salving of pain, but ..." Xe motions toward the operating theater, to include the collection of metal bed and gleaming instruments inside, the cascade of specialized miracles and bottled thaumaturgy. "Cold slows things down, even time. She'll give the chiurgeon wriggle room to work with. Get up. We will get something to eat. You don't want to be a nervous, famished mess when Lussadh's awake. Going to ruin that stoic-and-intense thing. Better be fed, well-rested, and polished for it. No?"

"I'm not hungry."

"Your body is. At the least you need alcoholic fortification. When the chiurgeon emerges with the good news we'll be the first to know, Ulamat will make it so."

Another person that she must do something about. That sobers her—anger firms the resolve—and she follows Guryin to one of the many dining rooms. There the table has already been set and the food is prompt. A servant sets up the kettle. Ghosts hiss as they wake to warm the pipes, power the stove to a low amber glow. "We'll handle ourselves for the rest." The major tosses the servant a gleaming, black-silver coin. "Thanks."

Guryin must have ordered the dishes ahead of time. There is a plate of glutinous rice cakes folded in bamboo leaves, another of chicken and beef satay, baskets of flatbreads and bowls of yellow, long-grained rice. Xe shows her the tea leaves. "I nicked this from the general. She won't mind. Occidental, I think. Very exotic. Listen—the general didn't do this. She forbade Ulamat from meddling and told him to send the monk home. I understand he meddled anyway."

The tea comes out a deep violet, exuding a hint of fruit, tart and foreign. Nuawa sips. "I see." And it does mean something, a load lifted. "I didn't think it likely of the general." Guryin may have reasons to dissemble, but she will believe it, for now.

The major tears a flatbread into strips. "What do you see yourself wanting from Lussadh?"

"I am glad for the attention she has seen fit to grant me. She was a prince; I have never been anything so lofty."

Guryin clicks xer tongue. "Give me a real answer."

"I have." She opens the pot on her half of the table. Red curry with veal, a variation on Lussadh's favorite. Something inside her wrenches. So much for the mirror shard's purification of the mind, that metamorphosis from helpless animal to an engine of rationality. She blinks. The tablecloth is spotted dark and damp; her tears have come without warning. "I'm ..." She tries to apologize for this break in manners, this loss of composure. Instead, the noise she makes is that of asphyxiation, a terrible rattling gasp. She presses her palms against her face.

The major steps around the table, putting a hand on her shoulder. "You'll get to have tea and curry with Lussadh again. I promise. Her Majesty, well. She is Her Majesty's heart."

"I'm not usually like this." Nuawa swallows and sucks in air and wipes uselessly at her face. "I am never like this."

"That I believe." Guryin offers her a kerchief.

They finish the food in relative silence, Guryin speaking on about xer betrothed, asking Nuawa if she has suggestions for the wedding and whether xe and Imsou could have a Sirapirat banquet. "In style, that is," xe says brightly. "Not so much in faith. I'm going to ask the general to officiate—you'll convince her, won't you? Much more fitting than any priest, Lussadh being the hierophant of winter, if you think about it. And you will dance with her at the party, her in red and gold, you in silver and blue. It will be magical, the two of you will be stunning."

Nuawa half-laughs, despite herself, her eyes still red and her nose still raw and her dignity still in tatters. "It's terrible manners to outshine the brides."

The major walks with her through the palace grounds, down the promenade that faces the Gate of Glaives. Xe points out a patrol trying to push a mobile barricade out of a frozen puddle. The queen is in residence and the climate has turned to obey. The air smells of imminent snowstorm. Frost lanugo has crept over the palace's pillars and collected on the edge of minaret roofs. It bleaches out the jewel colors of the spires, occluding them behind burial white.

In the suite, Nuawa is alone finally. The heating has to be turned higher, the ghosts churning harder, to maintain habitable temperature. She takes off her jacket, folds it into a neat square, hiding the blood. But preserving it as well. Royal blood, or blood that was royal once, whose letting reduces and halves Nuawa, makes her weak. Without the distraction of Guryin's chatter all she can see is that sanguine excess on the pavement, making a crimson bedspread beneath Lussadh; all she can see is Lussadh limp in the queen's arms, dyeing the queen that same shade.

From her shirt she draws the letter her mother left her. It has escaped the princely blood, remaining its pristine self. Such fine, expensive paper. The witching upon it too must have commanded a steep sum. She runs her fingers along the crisp edges, along the lines of green ink, the handwriting that she knows so well. Indrahi's house outside Sirapirat remains under her name, but she has not been back there since. Too much of a coward, despite everything. She hasn't kept the gun with which she executed her mother, either.

That house with its stripped trees, that conservatory with its persimmons.

Nuawa needs to make a copy, double-encode it, split the letter into fragments. She has memorized it, but memory is not a precise machine. It slips and betrays, creasing the fabric of truth.

For a long time, she clutches the letter, her eyes dry, her heart steady.

She tears the paper to pieces—the protection on it does not resist —and feeds the pieces to a lantern. They burn up easily. She turns the lantern off and taps out the cooling ashes into a dish, shielding it with her palm.

At the window she opens her hand and lets the gray flecks scatter. It is beginning to snow, and from the look of the sky, they will have a night of blizzard. Before she goes to sleep, she sends for Ulamat to request for her an audience with the queen.

————

FOR HER PART, Penjarej plays the terror-struck prisoner with what looks like born talent. The professor is wild-eyed, her head darting about, her breath steaming in the chill as she is escorted into the workshop. Each step, she is hardly steadier than a toddler, and she clutches her scarf and heavy robe to her as though they might confer protection.

Pretense or not, the abjection repulses Nuawa. She situates herself in the chamber that one of the queen's engineers have set up. It was a nursery once, for some royal child long gone to dust, and the ceiling glimmers with books. Volumes dangle from chains, covers made from hammered metal, pages from calcified fabric. Fables, she supposes, or lullabies or the other things that allegedly entertain children. She retains no recollection of what being a child was like.

She rises to greet Penjarej like a gracious, urbane host receiving an anticipated guest. Emulating the general, a little. "I trust my soldiers have treated you well, Professor?" She gestures to the tray of banana samosas, crispy and hot from the pan, drizzled with cardamom. "Please have some."

Penjarej waits until the soldiers who escorted her are gone before she digs in. From the look of her, it has been weeks—or more—since she had food this hot. When she has cleaned the plate and wiped her hand on a serviette, she raises her eyes to the worktable, the locked iron cabinet and the standing sarcophagus. The generous, uninterrupted space of the room with its trapezoid window.

"I belong even less here than the rest of the palace." Penjarej's robes are clean but worn, her jootis ragged.

"I'll have a better wardrobe arranged for you. The queen wants you kept in comfort."

"The queen—she's ... she's here?"

"Yes." Nuawa unlocks the sarcophagus. It is three or five times larger than a normal coffin and well-padded inside, velvet and satin, more luxurious than most people get in death. Scented with sandalwood and agarwood, as if it has been left next to burning incense.

In isolation, the god-engine Vahatma is small. Like Penjarej, it does not belong here, but for different reasons: the professor is too coarse, the god-engine is too fine. Vahatma is seated, holding a leopard in its lap, its two faces gazing forward at nothing. One face in meaningless peace, the other in impotent rage. Nuawa remembers her mother at this statue's knee, mangled and bruised, one arm bent and fingers broken. She never found out who did the torturing: the queen herself, some state official. The result on her mother was all she saw. Some nights, Nuawa dreams of the dry snap of fingers breaking, the rawness of a nail being pried off.

To the end, Indrahi did not give the queen anything.

"I have never seen Vahatma before." Penjarej's voice is hushed. "Not in person. Not actually."

"I have." Nuawa slides the cabinet open. In it, coils upon coils of mechanical parts. Spread out, they look impossible to fit into the god's shell. Cables like carotid arteries, pumps and bulbs that look pulmonary, gears larger than Nuawa's hands put together and teethed like an exquisite predator, all needle fangs. A nest of lenses fettered together, as though the god demands a hundred eyes for a hundred sights beyond this world. "Her Majesty's given me scant instruction. All she said was that she wants the god-engine activated."

"That's ... no easy task. Normally it'd need an entire team of engineers, mathematicians, a minor thaumaturge or two." The professor sorts through the components, her fingers passing over each; she is a little breathless, a votary meeting the object of her worship after a lifetime without. "Imagine if you were to fit yourself into a dress meant for a child. You'd get one arm through, at most. The god-engine is larger on the inside than the outside. The innards are altogether *too much*, but the original engineers were able to make it fit. So, transitive alchemy."

"The components were probably removed without much ceremony." She wonders if it was done in a rage, the queen tearing the chassis open with her bare white hands, ripping out the coils and intricate wheels with her bare white fingers. Those nails like talons, tearing the cables apart.

"Looks like so. They're all accounted for, I would say, the quantity matches my research. As for its activation—" Penjarej hesitates. "Even if the queen can assemble the right people who work well together, there's still the matter of the power source. As you might imagine, Lieutenant, this requires a lot more energy than a lamp."

"More ghosts than usual, then?" The queen owns an excess.

"Oh. No. It would need to be much *more*, a ghost that can function as the engine's animus. The ghost of something more potent than us, or the core of some mighty living machine." She pauses. "Like this palace."

Nuawa tries to imagine conveying this to the queen, and then the queen putting this question to Lussadh. By all accounts the palace is one of a kind, an entity of living architecture that responds to the al-Kattan blood alone. "That depends on how badly the queen wishes it. Can you infer what she wants with a god-engine?"

"It was built as a peerless defensive countermeasure. But it can be deployed as a siege weapon, an apocalyptic one." Penjarej spreads her hands. "I cannot begin to imagine what might be the target of her ire that she can't already ... admonish with her own will."

It is a fair point: the queen was able to defeat Vahatma. Perhaps her target is more abstruse, perhaps she has particular limitations. Nuawa files the thought away. "With this information, what do you think you could do, Professor?"

Penjarej meets her eyes. "As yet, not much. I am capable of assembling the parts, but I'll do nothing blunt."

Meaning she is not willing to obviously sabotage the engine and risk her own life for no reason. Until Nuawa finds out just what it is the Winter Queen requires. "And Ytoba?"

"Offered to severely hamper the queen. I found the thought compelling enough." The professor makes a cast-away gesture. "Ey also paid me in hard currency and I was on lean times. Ytoba already knew who I was. I could be turned in, or I could be paid and have a generous sum with which to run—to the occident, perhaps. But ey never did turn me in."

Nuawa thinks of informing Penjarej that she played a part in Indrahi's death, but that is not quite right, and it is ammunition best deployed strategically. Not now. She looks at the time and excuses herself.

The queen has summoned her to the southeastern minaret, a long way up by foot. The summit chamber is hexagonal, convex of ceiling, each side dominated by an oblong, tinted window. One damask, one blue, another pastel green, and yet another bleached amber. Each corner holds scrambled tiles. She finds the queen pushing at one such puzzle, turning each piece this way and that to no apparent avail. And Her Majesty somehow looks small. The bend of her spine, the plainness of her dress. Her brocade is half-layered, the color of a wet owl, so tousled that she might have gone to sleep in it and only recently woken up.

"If you turn the top-left one counter-clockwise three times and move the bottom-right one to the middle, Your Majesty," she says. The pane to her side gives a view of post-blizzard Kemiraj. Wilted banners and building facades swathed in silver. On one there is, barely visible, an image of the queen riding a chariot. Larger than life, in the most literal sense.

"Do I?" The queen doesn't look at her but follows her suggestion. The mosaic resolves into a tableau of a woman in armor, crushing pearls to dust under iron boots. She steps back from it. "How odd. It is meant to represent me, yet I feel no kinship to it at all. Do you know, I feel none to any of it, the images humans have made of me.

Monuments and paintings, murals and poetry. All that have nothing to do with me. Have you solved the mosaics before?"

She itches to ask, *What about the general, how is she?* But she will get her answer when she gets it, and she would've heard if Lussadh is dead. The operation must have been successful. "Not these ones, Majesty. But most of them work the same."

"An essential and predictable nature. Yes. It is unusual for you to seek me out. Do that mosaic for me, the one to the right."

She follows the queen's gaze to a panel between the yellow and pink windows. It has been scrambled thoroughly, and most of the tiles rotate in place as well as around, irregularly shaped. Some square, two isosceles triangles, a rhombus. But it is confined to the same rectangular frame, and she is quickly able to find the image's outline. It resolves into the same armored woman, that distant approximation of the queen, in a field of flowers as tall as her shoulders, massive red spider-lilies in riotous bloom.

The queen touches the mosaic, fingers running over the crimson petals. "They got the flowers right. These are for the dead, for souls bound to hell. Did I ever tell the artist about that? It's been some time since I took Kemiraj. It doesn't occur to me to remember these things. So, you've found my engineer."

"Yes. She claims you will need a source of great energy to activate Vahatma." This information comes out of her almost without her meaning to, pulling free as a rose-apple falls from a tree: answering gravity, not volition. *Slowly you will lose your will, become her creature in truth as well as pretense.* She stops herself short—she cannot unsay it, but she can change the subject. "I would ask about my reward."

A sound that is more trill than laugh. "The ruling of Sirapirat? How greedy you are; did I not say you'll need to wait a year or two? Patience. Yet I will reward you, yes, I will grant you marvelous gifts. An immaculate gun, an incomparable sword. Land, if you want that, or an arena of your own to entertain yourself with."

Nuawa's heart thumps. Now she stands at the edge of a cliff. "None of that, Majesty. I ask for your kiss."

The queen studies her with remote, ophidian regard. "What is it that motivates you? Simple ambition? Lussadh? Humans are far from difficult to comprehend, and then there's you, opaque as basalt. You resist domestication so well, ever you insist on being wild. A kiss. Is it that you seek to be Lussadh's equal?"

Nuawa folds her hands before her, holding herself carefully but meeting the queen's black gaze. This·is the way to deal with predators. "I don't wish to contest her place at your side, or her place in any other manner. But I remember what it was like to have your lips upon mine, and it has nothing to do with the call of the flesh."

"Did Lussadh tell you about my second benediction, or is it another of your astute deductions?" In the glacier geometry of the queen's face, the smile seems a fault-line. "Look at me. What do you see?"

"An arctic light and your eyes like stars burning."

"The Heron. How did he appear to you?"

There is an edge to the queen's question. It seems a non-sequitur, a peculiar thing to ask. "A naked figure, with wings from his back and hips and sides, and eider down his front. I would say he was hairless, as his body was covered in feathers. Very gaunt. I would judge him to be forty but it's hard to tell."

"Wings," the queen says softly. "You saw his wings."

The minutes lengthen. The queen does not appear even to breathe. Her inanimation is total—none of the stirring that signifies ongoing life, the respiratory rhythm, the miniscule movements that hint at coursing arteries and pumping atria.

"You should not have seen them. Even Lussadh perceived the Heron as human, shaped like you or her. The usual four limbs, the usual shape." The bathyal eyes examine Nuawa, pinpoints of light revolving within them. "The mirror does not grow in everyone the same. I woke your shard hardly months ago."

She has said too much, Nuawa realizes, has admitted more than she should. But there was no way to anticipate that she should have answered otherwise, to lie that to her the Heron was merely a man. "That is so, Your Majesty." What else remains for her to utter.

The Winter Queen takes hold of Nuawa, touching her belly, stopping at a point beneath her heart. Her hand drops. "The Heron," she says, "is alive. Piece by piece he reconstitutes himself. When I have found him, it will fall to you to hunt him down and bring me his heart. That shall be Vahatma's core, the piece of living puissance our engineer so demands. Prevail against him and you will have your kiss."

TEN

LUSSADH WAKES to the queen at her bedside. Her thoughts wheel sluggishly in place; she is on painkillers, likely an incredible quantity. The air is at once too bright and too dim, the sleet-light like pottery shards through the window. She is not in her bed. Ceiling too low, the stone too dark. "Your Majesty," she rasps. "I feel that I've failed you."

The queen strokes her jaw. "It does not reflect on you to face defeat before a creature such as that. A leaf is blown away by a storm, and who can fault the leaf?"

Despite her clouded cognition, she does not think herself a leaf. Her mouth is parched. "What was the Heron, my queen?"

"A vessel for might." The queen's gaze turns distant. "Container for a will. Once that was my will, for the most part. Now his container belongs to himself alone, though still he siphons from me. Strange how these things transpire. When I was made, I didn't have a consciousness to call my own. This array of intent and calculation you see today came about because I'd drawn a soul from its original body and kept it within me longer than I was meant to."

The painkillers make her say, "You never did tell me much of all that."

The mildest smile. "Why, my general, you never did ask. It is such an old, lengthy story. The age of a nation, the heft of a dynasty. In

Yatpun a war raged between the gods of the mountains and the mortals of the iron cities. I say gods and mortals, but the balance of power was more even than you might think. This tipped when the gods began to create my species. Snow-women the mortals would come to call us, though not all of us were female." Her head tips slightly. "We were sent into the wild as vacant dolls, without memory or desire. To the mortals we were like lost animals. Sometimes it was a seduction—they took us home to nurse to health, thinking us beautiful humans. Sometimes the draw was that we were innocent and fragile. Whatever the case, we would capture their souls. And souls, my treasure, are very potent. They transmute what they touch. Water flows to fit its vessel, but with souls it is the other way around."

Lussadh listens to the rhythms of her body. There is no fireplace in here—even if there was one, it'd have been extinguished in the queen's presence—and so the quiet is complete. The hum of ghosts is louder and closer, nearly rattling. She raises her head, not too far and reaches for the glass at her bedside, which she drains. Water tinged with lemon, of necessity chilled. Most things don't stay warm near the queen. "I can't imagine you as any other than what you are now."

The queen points to the floor, where snow begins to build into a mountain range, from which arises stone faces: anthropomorphic, but so severe that they are without expression. On the other side of the room, miniature cities spread across a moraine, their walls high and gleaming and delicate as frosting. Clouds of vehicles like tiny insects hover above them and rain down webs of gossamer snow, rime javelins and harpoons. "It's not a precise rendition," Her Majesty says, "us being indoor and there being hardly any space. Those mountains were the gods', those cities the mortals'. Do you see those, the flying things? I piloted one. My first flight was like nothing else I'd ever felt —I had no conception of mortality, no fear. But this was a test and most of these vehicles fell and my siblings with them. First, we were infiltrators to harvest souls, and then we were disposable shock troops." At a gesture from her the ice reforms: now there are behemoths, faceless and twice as large as the cities, with lashing serpentine limbs. They open their maws, swallow the cities down, and grind them to silver dust between teeth like boulders.

"The gods built siege engines the size of moving mountains and powered them with ghosts. They seared the mortals' mantled defenses and split open their iron cities. And so, the mountain gods won their war and gained dominion of Yatpun." The queen continues smiling. "By then my siblings and I were obsolete, the whole lot of us so fragile and ephemeral."

Lussadh doesn't need to prompt what happened after. She has lived her childhood and adolescence waiting for her grandaunt the king to decide which among the potential heirs would be worthy of succession. The rest were discarded, sometimes consigned to the executioner's blade. "I wonder," Lussadh murmurs, "what I would have done if I had chanced upon you in some white forest, snowed over, and you gazing up at me with eyes empty of knowledge. I like to think that I would have recognized the supreme transcendence in you, a glimpse of the divine."

"In Yatpun, there were fables of people who found my siblings and wedded them in gentleness and lived in bliss all the days of their lives." The queen snaps her fingers; the theater of ice and snow dissolves without a trace, not even water on the floor. She kisses Lussadh's brow. "Take off your robe."

Lussadh does. The wound is vast, a red and sanguine gate through her chest. The spear pierced her lung, must have bruised her kidney, and missed her heart by a hair: the tip of it was broader than most knives. Anesthetics keep her from feeling the profound damage on those connected structures inside her, the trachea and diaphragm, the river of esophagus and the arch of aorta. Blood in lumps and membranes clotting, which would have choked those passages if not for the salves that work to fortify her veins and smooth the flow of alimentary fluids. It will scar unlike any other injury she has ever sustained, both front and back, entry and exit.

The queen puts her mouth around the wound, exhaling lightly, the most feathery of sighs. Her eyes are shut in utmost concentration. The injury does not instantaneously heal but something much greater than a chiurgeon's craft occurs. The flesh is smoother where the queen has made contact, less raw. Lussadh breathes easier, heady with relief, the fog of painkillers lifting.

The queen stands and steps neatly out of her robe, the weight of fabric susurrating as it falls to pool at her feet. It is a stunning sight, a vision, and no matter how many times she has seen this, it never fails to stir Lussadh. The small breasts, the skin that seems less like flesh and more like lantern-glass for the luminescence that dwells within, the swell of hips against the starkness of it all. Knots of wiry hair at armpits and between thighs, making odd shadows. The queen gestures at herself, one hand passing up from her stomach to her chest. "How many spirits do you think I contain, Lussadh?"

"As many as you require. No fewer, and no more."

The queen laughs. "It is my nature to kill what I love."

"That describes a lot of us, my queen."

"Were I to kiss you a third time, Lussadh, I'd simply kill you. Glass-bearing or not your animus would freeze and sink into me, like a piece of shipwreck into the sea. The mouth is the conduit of souls, their natural exit." She climbs back into the bed, onto Lussadh's lap. Her hand grazes Lussadh's belly, low, then lower. "The mirror was also my heart, and when I crossed the barrier from there to here, it tumbled out of me and split to pieces. So many. One of them is inside you and I could give you more still, to strengthen you, to make you more than mortal."

"That's what you did for the Heron. It changed him." Lussadh moves, slightly; she cannot remain quite still, not with the queen's hand on her like this, all her blood concentrating in one place, one spot.

"Correct. And he grew greedy. Why stop at two fragments of my mirror, when he could steal three, four, five ..." The queen's fingers apply more pressure, stroke a little faster. "I've thought of inviting Nuawa here. To have her cradled between us, writhing helpless, crying out wildly like a hawk as we make her come again and again."

Her breath catches. She is almost impossibly hard, more than she has any right to be with her injury so fresh. And yet. "Yes."

The queen pushes her down. Her cunt is slick and cool as she lowers herself onto Lussadh, the grip of it like nothing else. The queen rises and falls; the bed creaks under them.

"Come inside me," the queen whispers, "I want to feel your heat deep in me and it will be like a small, incandescent annihilation."

And she does, and it is.

For a time, they are in silence, joined, the queen still above her and bent like a bow. The royal face is flushed the same way storm clouds may stain the sky, the starbursts of her eyes enormous. "I'll tell you my name. In all this country, in all the world beyond the island of my birth, you'll be the only one to know."

She leans down and speaks into Lussadh's ear, and her name sinks into Lussadh like a pilgrim into the slow-moving dunes.

———

THE QUEEN'S instructions come sooner than Nuawa anticipated, while she is overseeing Penjarej in the makeshift atelier. It is delivered not by Ulamat or calling-glass, but by a snow-maid.

Penjarej screams as the snow-maid climbs in through the window, moving with the satiny ease of an invertebrate. But when it lands it looks as human-like as ever, wearing the same alien smile it always does. Petite frame, slender limbs, and eyes like the queen's: black irises, black sclera, the gaze of deep-sea animals. Made in the image of the queen's siblings, Nuawa now recognizes, either to mock or commemorate.

The snow-maid comes up to her and points at its bare breasts, its bare stomach. On these surfaces is a map to an old crematorium not far from Kemiraj's boundaries: a smear of black on paper-white flesh. More instructions, written raggedly around a sketch of disintegrated architecture.

"I understand." Nuawa inclines her head, knowing she is the only one who can see the queen's missive. The snow-maid nips her hand like a curious dog before exiting the way it entered.

"Oh, gods." Penjarej hurries to double-bolt the window and drop the shutters. For good measure, she leans against the frame. "What was that?"

"A royal courier." The crematorium is a few hours' travel by carriage. Best to leave within the day. "I'll be absent for a time. My colleague Major Guryin will be overseeing you. Xe's very charming and a staunch defender of winter."

The professor nods her understanding: no more needs to be said.

Nuawa stops by her suite to retrieve the anthurium pendant in its little box, delivered this morning by the jeweler. She stays there for a while, turning the velvet case this way and that, scrutinizing its flawless integument.

Crossing the wing to Lussadh's sickroom, she feels pursued, that behind her something is biting and licking at her shadow. The closer she gets, the more this sensation mounts.

The general's voice comes through—*Enter*—before she even knocks. So much for stalling.

She finds Lussadh reading by the window, a small black book in hand, nude. The general looks for all the world like the erotic inspiration for a sculpture, one that might be called *Contemplation* or *The Soldier-Scholar*. Alabaster lighting glazes and softens the contours of the general's body, yet there's no obfuscating the serpentine curve of the spine, the narrow hips and thick thighs that Nuawa has many times traced with her tongue.

"I thought you would come to see me sooner," Lussadh says. "I have been on my feet for days, Lieutenant. The chiurgeon doesn't even fuss over me anymore."

"I had—" Work to do, a task assigned by the queen, but those are only excuses. "General, I could have been someone else. You are not wearing anything."

Lussadh turns to her, shutting the book—Nuawa catches the title, *Verses from the Frontline*, a collection once included in many curricula, fallen since out of favor because it engages too closely with insurgency, with the romance of fugitive lives. "I knew it was you," the general says. "Remember, I have a better sense of glass-bearers than most. You especially."

Nuawa picks up a robe Lussadh has carelessly flung to the foot of the bed. She drapes it over the general, though it covers no more than those muscled shoulders, that long shapely back. "I needed the time to think."

"About what?" This is asked softly.

"It was my fault that you left the palace. By rights, I should have taken the spear for you." It is merely the correct thing to say. More than anyone, Nuawa knows she does not believe in most of what she speaks. But the words come out of her without premeditation, as though propelled by conviction like a tide.

"By rights, I do not deserve to have your death. I myself made the decision to come after you, and I hear you held the Heron at bay most admirably."

Nuawa touches the general's neck. The pulse there burns under her fingertips like a living coal. "Lieutenant Guryin admonished me. Xe wanted to know whether I have—that is, if I ever ..."

"Not an inappropriate question, I trust?"

"No. Of course not. Xe suggested I could stand to be more ... open, more forward with what I mean." Nuawa puts the velvet box in the general's palm. "This is as nothing next to what you're used to, a trifle."

Lussadh opens the box, lightly touches the felt and peels it away to reveal the pendant. A silver anthurium, plated against tarnishing, with a spadix of sanded rose gold. Her smile softens all of her, her features, the set of her shoulders. "It is far more sublime to me than any pearl. Not as sublime as you, but what is? Put it on for me."

She does so on tiptoes, brushing hair away and fastening the clasp at the nape of Lussadh's neck. Then she puts her mouth against the base of the general's skull. "On that day, I thought what it'd be like if I couldn't wake up beside you or have dinner with you again. Is that not maudlin and childish?"

"When I was very young, I'd have thought so. I like to think I've learned better since." Lussadh turns around and draws her toward the bed. On each other they lean, arm to arm. "Shall we trade stories of our youth? Though I haven't been young for a long time, whereas for you such stories are not too distant."

"From what your body tells, I would never know. You're so hale and so—mighty." Nuawa takes off her shoes and draws her legs up into the nest of heavy pelts. Lussadh always piles those up for her sleep, a preference for animal hide with iron weight over soft fabric. "I feel like an unruly adolescent, secretly stealing away to a sweetheart's bed. Not that I ever got to do such a thing."

"Can it be that you weren't courted at that age?"

How easy it is to tell true stories and yet never the truth. "My aunt said the countryside children were beneath me in intellect and education; I believed her. I'd killed my first wolf long before I'd gotten my first kiss. Actual bedding—I was twenty-seven. I had just won my first major match, and one of the spectators was this woman with eyes I liked."

"A champion may have her pick. Fitting." Lussadh has tied her robe shut, though it still leaves much of her chest bare, the anthurium now glinting on her breast like a shuttered sun. "My first lover was from Shuriam. We were of an age, seventeen, and she'd tell me of her country: a land of bone fastnesses and ivory sentinels. As it happens, she was also a saboteur and a spy. My grandaunt had me execute her and Shuriam invaded. We annexed it three years after. This was to teach me a lesson in strength, in power and in who wields it. And that those weakened by sentiment do not deserve to."

Nuawa teases stray hair out of the pendant's chain. "Is that why you bargained with the queen?" Already Nuawa is thinking of how to edit her own past to echo the general's, to embellish or lessen to engineer common ground. And perhaps that is what all lovers do, embroidering and snipping their individual threads until they march in unison, in rank and file as infantry does.

"No. Or rather not the whole of it." Lussadh winces as she reaches for her bedside table—the wound troubling her still, despite her assertion that she is now at ease—and brings a platter over. Baked gold drops, marzipan fruits, coconut crisps. "The whole of it was, where did I stand in the king's regard? How much choice did I have to not serve my birthright? I desired option. Of course, I do govern Kemiraj now, and so Ihsayn had her way, in the end."

She looks at the platter between them, at the glitter of sugar and yolk, at the luster of glazed marzipan. Sirapirat desserts. There, then, a lover's thoughtfulness, to have this delivered from some Sirapirat confectioner. It might even have come on the same train that carried her brother's casket. Lussadh's tenderness, her brother's carcass. The question is not which weighs more, but what scale to use. "What would you have chosen, left to your own devices?"

The general laughs, the sound like new-smelted platinum, precious and coruscant. "I have never thought about it deeply. I would say a glassblower; how marvelous it would be to work with a substance so fascinating, but I don't have the finesse. A florist then. To have a glasshouse larger than this room and fill it with anthuriums, bromeliads, snapdragons. Then a basin of lotuses and cattails, and water irises."

"When I can afford one—" She does not think of Indrahi's persimmons. "I'll buy you just such a glasshouse, and we'll see if you can make things grow."

"And you'll have to watch me fumble through sacks of fertilizers and watering cans, and I'll press upon you stunted water irises that didn't grow quite right."

"Every last one I will treasure all the same and press dry between books to preserve." Nuawa fits herself against the curve of the general's arm, the line of the general's flank, and closes her eyes. How easy, after all. The correct scale all along is forgetting.

When Lussadh has fallen asleep, Nuawa gently extricates herself and for a time watches the general rest. Then she turns aside. She has been tasked with a hunt, and there's no time to waste.

ELEVEN

LUSSADH GIVES herself one more evening to recuperate before she puts herself to statecraft. Despite four decades of practice, it remains something she has to prepare for, the way one works up to a lengthy run or a climb up sheer, high cliffs. The details, the moving parts, the hinges on which decisions turn. The inescapable notion that she is merely assuming King Ihsayn's role, for all that she promised Kemiraj a reign more just, a reign more equitable. Ideals wither before the ravages of reality.

She goes through the minor matters first, the ones Ulamat has filtered for her. A note that the monk's body has been sent to the Seven Spires for the bhikkuni Kabilsingh to tend. Next, a schedule for removing the barricades and returning the city to civil law, now that the Heron has been disposed of. She puts her signature on a stack of documents, then a stack of letters. Her pen is running out of the chrome ink that makes forging her sigil difficult. Governance is ultimately mundane, whatever load of titles one carries about like the train of an impractical dress.

"Veshma," she says without looking up. "Thank you for coming. I can always count on your punctuality."

The minister quietly sits. Lussadh half-expects her to draw a gun, bare a knife. But Veshma is the same Veshma as ever, prim and a complete stranger to force of arms. But the look in her eyes is familiar, the same one in Sareha's before the old woman unsheathed her machete. This look is beyond bargaining or intimidating: like Sareha, Veshma has made her choices and is at peace. She can no more be disturbed or reasoned into guilt than a sarcophagus can.

Lussadh spins the pen across her fingers, a whirl of red wood and metal cap. "I never used to think of politics as limited by stationery supplies. Yet here I am, unable to sign the next thing because I'm running low on an ink. We're thwarted by such trivialities. What do you think?"

"I have no opinion, my lord."

"Do you," she says, conversational, "miss King Ihsayn? Sun-Bearer, Ghazal of Conquest, the final king of Kemiraj. She really did have striking titles."

Veshma turns her gaze to one of the masks. A plain one, made of white rice paper layered over a rattan frame, with small perked nose and mouth. "No, my lord. The dead are not for missing. They have other purposes entirely."

"Now you sound like a fakir." She takes the mask from its hook on the wall and offers it to Veshma, who recoils as though it could transmute into a bouquet of thorns, a goblet of poison. "No? Fair enough. These are eccentric items to collect. On to the matter at hand. I think you were as surprised at what happened at the feast as I was. Fortunately, I am blessed with access to expertise on this specific subject. After I learned how such alchemical violence came to be, I thought and thought, how strange—a shard of the queen's mirror cannot be slipped into food like a toxic seed, a pinch of venomous petals. It's a very intentional act and, I suspect, quite painful. To have a piece of glass, not small, inserted into you. Sedated or not, it would leave a mark."

The minister does not avert her gaze. Her composure is comprehensive.

Lussadh returns the mask to its place; it rustles in her hand, a fragile moth-noise. "The mirror pieces don't take in all soil." So the queen said. "It can reject the flesh in which it's been planted, to disastrous result. As you yourself have seen. I don't know what the Heron said the queen's glass would do for you, grant you the powers he wielded perhaps? Mostly it let him dictate the hour of your death, provide a conduit through which he could spy on me when he couldn't pierce the palace's wards. Small wonder he knew my comings and goings so well. I assume he had you poison Lieutenant Nuawa." To remove a glass-bearer.

"He never did say why he wanted her gone. I suppose I'll be dying soon."

"Not so abruptly as Juhye did." Had the shard taken root and marked Veshma as a viable glass-bearer, this conversation would have gone in quite another direction. "You're taking it well. However one is born—of the enamel or elsewise—the fire of Kemiraj flows through all of us. It smelts our spirit harder than any steel. We have our pride. You're Kemiraj to the end, and I respect that."

"Had you ruled this country in your own right," Veshma says abruptly, "it would have been different. We thought that you would sit the throne—formally, informally, what did it matter—and govern this land we've given ourselves to. Instead we got an official content to work on the Winter Queen's behalf, remaining here but rarely, running Her Majesty's errands abroad and conquering in her name. Sareha had reasons of her own, but ours arose because we believed in you. You the symbol, you the person. The pride of our prince."

She brings order to her desk. She holds up a stack of papers, taps the edge against the table until the entire stack is as perfectly aligned as a marble slab. She gathers up her pens and pencils and puts them in their holder. Once the disarray is gone, what is left behind is the emptiness of a new-made map, borders not yet drawn, territories not yet inked. "I promised justice. I promised liberty from my grandaunt's hand. Both of these I have delivered. What you and Juhye and the rest wanted is not what I sought; it never was. As long as I breathe, I'll guide Kemiraj, but I will not be shackled to a throne or ruled by a crown."

"Then," the minister says, "the Kemiraj we fought for is dead."

"The country continues. With luck, what we've established will persist beyond our lifetime." Indeed, Her Majesty, being immortal and inclined to let Kemiraj run as Lussadh wishes, guarantees the fact.

Winter is bulwark against change, against corruption of Lussadh's legacy. "Kemiraj is Kemiraj. I've secured this to the best of my ability, Veshma."

Veshma stands and collects stray papers that, despite Lussadh's efforts to keep tidy, have fallen from her desk. She is meticulous. "I remember when you were a child," she says as she works, "how solemn you were and how you made it look effortless to meet King Ihsayn's standards. To anyone with a working eye it was obvious who'd rise to be heir. And some of us could see, too, that becoming Ihsayn's ideal caused you pain. You were a tender child."

"On the contrary I was an ambitious one, a hungry one." Yoked to the need to be the last one standing more than anything.

The minister straightens and presents to her a daguerreotype, framed, that's fallen to the floor and lain buried beneath office detritus. It is old, an outmoded thing from before images could be recorded in color. It shows a group of children standing uneasily together in two files. Some tall, some short, all with the al-Kattan look. "You don't need to forget everything, my lord. And now I ask for a boon. Let us—Juhye, myself, the others—enter history as we were, as the ones who've been there with you from the beginning. You owe us at least that."

"I do." Lussadh retrieves from one of her drawers a small vial. "I do owe you that."

Veshma gazes deep into the vial, at the sap-thick poison, a formula perfected for painless death. Meant exclusively for al-Kattan use: there were a multitude of reasons a member of the family might require a fast end. Failing the king, trespassing against the strictures placed on all who bear the name, bringing shame to the throne. "Might I have something to wash this down with?" Veshma asks. "I hear it's saccharine. I've never liked sweet things."

Wordlessly Lussadh opens her liquor cabinet and fetches her bitterest vodka. She pours a cup three-quarters full, adds two drops of the al-Kattan toxin, and thinks back to when she contemplated swallowing it herself. Straight from the vial, undiluted, a clog of sugar thickening in her throat until she could no longer breathe. It was not during moments of stress or fear; rather she considered this in times of idleness, when she was entirely rational and calm. More than anything, living like that under Ihsayn convinced her to take that irrevocable step, sent her to the Winter Queen.

"Here," she says and slides the cup toward Veshma. "I'll remember you fondly, and any will you've drawn up I shall honor. Your kin will not be wanting. Rest well."

The minister drinks without flinching and drains the cup of every drop.

In hardly any time at all, Veshma slumps in the seat, eyes shut and limbs slack. Lussadh gazes into the distance—her window affords her a stunning view, this view of the city that dwells within her heart and occupies her dreams. The jeweled architecture, the soft mist that rises at dawn, the bridges that clasp like lovers' hands.

Is it weakness, she thinks, to want company now; to not have to stand here alone and remember where she misstepped? To confront her faults in all their sordid hierarchy, examining each by each like a piece of faulty clockwork.

There is the queen, all-giving, all-permissive. Then there is Nuawa, who is neither of those things.

Back in her sickroom, the palace chiurgeon is ready to clean her wound and change her dressings. They ignore as best they can that the Winter Queen stands in a corner, vigilant, a scrim of frost like opals radiating from her bare heels. The chiurgeon remarks that Lussadh is healing fantastically and that she'll be good as new in no time; she thanks the chiurgeon and sends them on their way.

"The chiurgeon's hands were shaking." The queen sweeps her foot over the buildup of rime, a dainty gesture, and makes it disappear. "Humans scare too easily."

"Their hands were steady enough during the operation and I'm in fine trim. Mostly thanks to you, but chiurgeons have their uses." Lussadh pulls the queen to her, stroking down one long, glorious leg and nuzzling a slim hip with her mouth. "Have you seen Nuawa about?"

"She's elsewhere. Your lovely lieutenant asked me for a precious prize, and I mean to make her earn it."

"What might that have been, greatest of queens? Nuawa's usually modest in her wishes." A promotion in rank or an estate seems unlike the lieutenant to request. Power in Sirapirat, plausibly.

"It is a closer, more personal thing. Very ... avaricious. She's full of hidden desires."

Something in the words, something about the way this is said, stops Lussadh short. "What duty has she been set to?"

Her queen does not often hesitate. There is half a beat before she says, "Nuawa is out hunting the Heron. What is left of him."

Lussadh looks up into those deep, ocean-trench eyes. "Your Majesty, you've never been false with me. Is the Heron still dangerous? Is he capable of harming her?"

"Your lieutenant is dangerous in her own right. She is currently alive."

"Where has she gone?"

The queen does not blink. "I could forbid you to seek her out."

"My queen," she says softly, "when I entered your service, we made a covenant. King Ihsayn made me kill my lovers to affirm my loyalty to the throne. You promised that you would never test me that way."

"Yes." The queen takes one step away, not far, but it is a withdrawing. She winds together her perfect fingers, each tipped in nails that are slightly blue, as though they have been lacquered. But it's merely her natural color, part of the luminescence that flows under her skin. "In my making, there shouldn't even have been a component capable of this. You're my weakness, Lussadh. The one person to whom I can deny nothing."

"Please."

"The Heron has gone to lick his wounds in that old crematorium. You remember it well."

The place where she first properly met the queen. Lussadh passes her hand over her wound-dressing to make sure it is secure and starts putting on warm clothes. She locates her weapons—the gun with its conventional bullets, ones that stand a chance of scratching the Heron—and straps them on. "I will be back swiftly, Your Majesty."

"See that you do." The queen has turned away. Ice crackles and hisses as it rapidly wraps the windowsill, branching into fractal wings

—crane and crow, hawk and hummingbird. "I shall not forgive your failure to return in perfect condition."

———

THE MILITARY CARRIAGE takes Nuawa to a point half a day's walk from the crematorium. Any closer and she might alert the Heron too soon. She has eaten before she came, though the food—fine as it was, cooked by the best chef in the palace—left no lasting taste. She has brought dried fruits and meats, just in case.

What was once desert spills out around her, gray and occasionally patched with sickly moss. She hears from Guryin that this land was much more dangerous once, the dunes inhabited by predatory wind-lynxes with a taste for human flesh. They died out, unsuited to the new climate, the new order. Nuawa has thought that the presence of cold should have rejuvenated the sand, shifting barren tracts to fertile, making meadows of sand-bitten crags. Perhaps this is possible on the furthest borders, but for most of Kemiraj's territory there must be a fundamental incompatibility, a land that's known emptiness for so long nothing can grow upon it.

In the distance, the crematorium looms and she is surprised to find familiar features: naga scales, finials, a spire that once vented smoke. Nobody in Kemiraj ever burned their dead—too wasteful—and instead gave corpses to carrion eaters. There must have been Sirapirat presence here, once.

When she reaches them, she finds the walls wrecked, reduced to stubby outcrops like pulverized teeth. The spire is shorter than Kemiraj minarets, dressed in stone the color of old skulls and trimmed with faded curlicues.

She walks steadily through the snow, which outside civilization is allowed to accrue, piling up and up: it is as high as her knees, though soft and loose, like wading through sawdust. Easy now to see what her mothers did, that snow erases and turns what it touches into a copy of itself. Her breath curls out. It has been so long since she has been outside a city, longer still since she has had only herself for company. By nature, she is solitary, and she has forgotten that in the push-pull of Sirapirat, the fumes of the tournament, and then the general. The general most of all, who has made her misplace herself.

Nuawa sets her face against the low, susurrating wind. She half-expects to hear animal cries, but there are only the currents of the air and the flattened, empty sky. Still this is closer to the landscape of her adolescence than she has ever been in for decades, the countryside where she stalked the trails of bears and wolves. Bears more than wolves, those being unsocial and easier to bring down, not running in packs. She remembers the first time she tracked one to its den and shot it in the head, the wet heat of blood steaming on stone. Already the iteration of her that wept over Lussadh seems apart and distant, not really her at all. It is the Nuawa from before, young and running like she is born to the tundra, that is the true essence.

A ruined monastery is attached to the crematorium, worn down entirely, shredded as if someone specifically demolished it. Roof absent, walls done with. A few jagged spaces that used to be monks' sleeping chambers. She spots a dot of red on the white ground and thinks that it is blood, but it's only a fragment of detritus that once brightened some pillar. She puts it back down, where it gleams in the frost like a single jewel in a filigree the size of eternity.

Past a broken gate, she surveys the smaller buildings that ring the crematorium. A shed or two. A central column where offerings were left: bronze and brass bells whose tongues have long rotted off, a collection of singing bowls that have lost both their gleam and music. It surprises her that these remain at all—they should be a fine bounty to historians and archeologists. But perhaps the scholars of Kemiraj, before winter or otherwise, think Sirapirat's precursor or offshoots beneath notice. They thought themselves the greatest before the Winter Queen came, and now they think themselves the finest still, beloved and ascendant.

Nuawa strains her ears. After more than a decade in Sirapirat her senses for such things have tarnished, and she's no longer as alert to the rustling in the leaves and the scraping of claws on snow. But her quarry is not a wolf or a bird of prey. People are much easier to find, on balance, than deer or bear cubs. So far, she has spotted no sign of the Heron. He may not need heating so she hasn't been looking for fires, yet some fraction of him must remain human, answer to human needs—shelter, food, sleep.

Eventually she sees it, a red print turning the brown of dead leaves. She kneels and takes off her glove to touch, sinking her finger into the damp. This time it is not a stray pebble.

The trail is not fresh, but it is steady, uninterrupted. A drop of russet, another drop. Up she goes on crumbled steps, to the first, then the second floor of the main building. Her footfalls are loud in the purity of absence, the stasis of ruin. She encroaches.

On the third floor, among decayed pallets and dissolved furniture, the corpse of a pig sprawls. It has been slaughtered hastily, torn down the middle the way a stuffed toy might be ripped by a tempestuous child. For an animal so crude and filthy there is hidden elegance to the symmetry of its ribs, those refined parabolas doubling in on themselves. The Heron does need to eat, after all. There is not much left inside the pig: the offal has been devoured, even the brain has been gouged out for sustenance, the skull scraped until it shines like expensive ivory.

A day old, two at most.

She replays the snap of throat, the impact of body on hard sediment. But she was not around to watch what occurred after. Maybe he pulled himself back together piece by piece. Bones knitted, tendons reformed, those wings retracted. And then he stole a pig from some city pen and brought it to this fort to fall upon like a ravenous dog.

Even in his state, he can still move. Track him by the things that seem to you a trick of refraction, the things that should not be there, that you believe are products of an unsteady mind. Track him by the traces and prints that you alone can see. Those will lead you to the Heron.

Much as it galls to follow the queen's instructions, she has no alternative. Nuawa shuts her eyes and lets herself drift, emptying her thoughts. When she opens them again, she begins to see it, the places where air fractures and an opal radiance leaks through. Like phosphenes they are not truly there, a phenomenon visible to her eyes and no other, hallucinogenic. Sometimes it flickers out and she finds something else, frost flowers that have formed where there is no plant to give them skeleton, feathers that are too long and large to belong to any bird. She picks one up, turns it in her hands to see the daylight run rainbow along the vane. The quill is harsh white, with a wan undercurrent of gold.

The trail starts and stops, or rather her senses fall out of synchronization with it. She approximates the direction as she leaves the crematorium, keeping west with an eye out for landmarks: some rock formations ahead, jutting black out of the white. Now she can hear birds—very distant, either a repopulation that ran away from the city or some miraculous species that survived the transition from desert to tundra.

The day bleeds out, losing gradually all the brightness from its veins. By then Nuawa has entirely lost the trail, and no amount of remaining still and letting her vision haze will regain the Heron's track. She locates a copse of stone and a place to shelter beneath them. She covers herself with the extra coat she brought—warm enough, though it shouldn't be, in this weather. She does wonder at these changes, what would happen to them when the queen is no more: would the shard simply thaw and dissolve, or would it burst through her cardiac valves. All of them—Guryin, Lussadh, Nuawa—it would kill, and no skill at arms or thaumaturgy would stop the fact. Winter's end would be instantaneous, not just its monarch but its commanders, the heads of its army. Nuawa has not mulled on this before, what lies beyond her immediate future, the potential aftermath should she succeed.

She huddles in her coats and studies the small, yellow flowers that have managed to find foothold here. The stone above her is draped in lichen in burnt orange, in anemic gray.

In the morning, she eats her strips of cured pork, a length of dry sweet sausage, red and shot through with fat. She drinks out of a copper bottle: no time to melt the snow. Slowly she rises, chasing the stiffness out of her joints and stretching until she is sure her muscles are limber, and she is quick on the draw of the gun or the blade.

The dawn brings with it a return of the Heron's mark, a flicker in the corner of her eye, a ringing of bells. She turns to that and follows on.

Another outcrop of crags and boulders that look as though giant hands have stacked them into precarious, uneven towers. Beneath one such formation, Nuawa finds him. The Heron curls fetal in a shroud of his own feathers, the wings furled high and tight. They are as whole and exquisite as they were on that roof, perhaps even more. The wing-span is broader, the plumage brighter, the tips of primary feathers shining as though they have been dipped in rose gold and mercury.

She keeps her distance and keeps her gun out of its holster. Quietly she says, "Man from Yatpun."

One of the smaller wings at his hip twitches, but there is no other response. She takes a step closer. "In Sirapirat you met two women and you left them a shard of glass. Do you remember?" She speaks slowly, clearly.

A tremor of feathers. The wings part and she sees that his face is hardly human. It was gaunt before; now it is a skull, and from the sides of his neck extend sharp, thin beaks like a hummingbird's. His throat bends at an odd angle, not entirely recovered from the queen's strength. His eyes have gone strange, the dark of pupils leaking into the white of sclera, and when his gaze darts around rather than at her she sees that his sight is either lost or severely impaired. He opens his lips and a rattle comes out. He gathers a fistful of snow with a trembling hand and pours it into his mouth. As his throat labors to swallow it she thinks, *This is my test, the monster I've been sent to kill.* Yet all that remains is a terrible ruin.

The consequence of stealing power and wielding it without permission: perhaps that is what the queen wants Nuawa to bear witness, not a test but a warning.

The glob of snow disappears, and he licks his lips, mouth twisting as though trying to reacquaint itself with speech. He turns his head this way and that, and she hears the crunch of bones warping. In a moment his neck is straight, almost unmarred save for the imprint of the queen's hand. It did not bruise—there is no blood in him to bloom beneath the skin—but there is a dark blemish all the same, vivid and blue. "You," he croaks. "Ytoba should have brought you."

Her pulse jumps. "Ytoba." The Heron has not, quite, said it but she can already guess. And that would mean—

"Ey was to bring you to me. The prize I sought. Fate is a peculiar tide. Ey and I could never have crossed paths, yet something between us pulled, aligned ..."

Nuawa stares down at him, at this architect of misfortune. Whether he meant it or not, he set into motion all of this. First Tafari. Then Indrahi. He does not seem aware of—or alarmed by —her gun.

His tongue laps at the air, as if to taste her scent. Like the rest of him, the tongue is as colorless as dead scars. "I remember it now. I know what you are after and we share a common goal. Your mothers, they gave this glass to you, didn't they? I can see it in you, a seed that's harbored in the richest soil, piercing soul after soul. Now with you it has grown to fullness, a fruit at last ready for the reaping."

Nuawa blinks, trying to force her eyes to see it again the tributaries of radiance running over his skin. Right now, he seems only flesh, wings or not. "That was your purpose? To plant the mirror shards and come back for them when they were ripe?" Piercing soul after soul. How many glass-bearers have held this exact sliver of mirror.

"Do you not desire the queen's fall?" He extends a hand covered in eiderdown, pallid and cadaverous. "Give me your heart. Your piece."

"Didn't you tell my mothers that the queen becomes mortal at the moment of her kiss? You, I have a feeling, won't be able to persuade her to that gesture." Drawing him out, pushing to see if she can extract more answers. Whatever else, that must be paramount.

"I could, once." His mouth stretches, baring teeth and gums the hue of ash. "She may become breakable flesh for that one instant, but you're insufficient, child. You are not mighty—her mirror is—and that has fooled you into believing you are more than its vessel."

She studies his near-blind eyes, his desiccated stomach. A husk of foiled schemes. "Then there's nothing more to discuss." She levels her gun.

The Heron's grin stretches wider and he raises his hand, clenching it into a fist. "The mirror links us all, child of Sirapirat. In one like you, whose mirror has matured so well, the sympathy between you and me tugs like a fishing line. Watch."

Nuawa's hand moves in tandem with his, as if he is the person and she the reflection. This happens without her—she does not even feel it, the flexing and undulating of tendons, the intricate mechanisms that animate even the simplest human motion. She stares down as her treasonous hand returns her gun to its holster. She tries to resist, but there is nothing to push against, no force with which to contend. There is only a searing chill that radiates from her chest. Her heart pounds and it is as though her body has gone hollow, an acoustic chamber for cardiac percussion.

"By and by I came to learn that a single mortal body can bear no more than a single shard. It is not the quantity then, but the quality. One potent fragment of *her* mirror is better than a dozen weak ones, and taking that potent piece on I'll come very, very close to being her equal. I thought the glass in her favorite general was my answer. But yours. Yours is the one I planted myself, and how it has grown ..." He sweeps his arm—hers follows—a theatrical flourish to show his control is absolute. "Where you will fail, I shall succeed. All the burden you bear that you inherited from your mothers, it shall be put right. I can be your vengeance."

She bats uselessly against the possessed arm, hitting it hard enough to bruise. "Why do you seek the queen's fall?" Stalling. "You were her first retainer."

"Perhaps she did not grant me my dues. Perhaps I came to disagree with her goals. Simply because you are dying does not entitle you to revelations, child of Sirapirat. Even ghosts may rise up once more and disgorge secrets. There are many arts in the world, and most of them traffic in the dead. The fabric of existence is stitched by souls."

Her sword has left its sheath. He makes her brandish it, swing it through the air as though sparring against a phantom opponent. The blade-shadows splay out, wild writhing shapes like the lashes of a whip. One laps at her. A gash opens in her hip, hot and thick. Blood steaming in the snow, the smell of butchery.

The Heron rolls his wrist. Her trapped hand spins the blade, the way she might if she's putting on a show for the arena. The steel whistles as it cleaves through the air. "Had we met sooner. Something might have come out of it. But you hardly seem the sort to serve as a tool. You think yourself a force of your own, a free agent—" He reverses his grip.

Nuawa twists away, dodging her own blade. It grazes her coat, a bright, sharp line above her breast. "I'm not so hubristic as that." She is almost choking on her own breath and spit. To anyone watching it must be a farcical sight. "A spy in the queen's palace—" She grits her teeth. A thought emerges, between the thunderclaps of her panic. "I could do much for you."

"Reduced to begging after all? But no. I have waited for tenfold longer than you've been alive—more. It is time I take the fight to her. And to do that I require your part of her heart." He adjusts the angle of his arm, the direction of the sword. But he takes his time, relishing the control, the power that allows him to forget the state of his physical coil, the ruin in which he abides.

His savoring gives her time to draw her gun and fire it, point-blank, into her left wrist.

She has never seen so much of her own blood, and she has spent nearly two decades in arenas. It douses everything: her legs, her front, the Heron. Her sword falls and its shadows gutter out. The Heron recoils, capable of shock after all.

He still looks surprised when she shoots him in the face.

"I am," she whispers, "my own vengeance."

The instant he goes limp, pain comes in full force. Her eyes stream; her vision warps and the world is as seen through a concave glass. Still she fires into him.

The gun clicks empty. On her knees she retches; when she tries to support her weight on the shattered wrist it draws all her nerves into that one point, the entirety of her a single concentration of agony. Her stomach cramps and bile gurgles out of her.

She blacks out and comes to intermittently. When she finally has hold of her consciousness again, she is facedown in snow soaked in blood and vomit. Her breath is sour, filthy; she spits it all out. The Heron has not moved, has not made a second miraculous recovery. He lies in his own collapse, covered in a funeral shroud of stained feathers.

She crawls on her knees toward him, panting. With her good hand she picks up her sword and turns to the corpse. The only way to be sure is to carve out the Heron's heart. Through the reek of her own waste and in the heat of her own blood, she sets to work.

———

LUSSADH DOES NOT BRING A MAP; she does not require one. The terrain around the imperial city is as familiar to her as the lines of her palm, the topography of her history. It may be buried under snow, but this was once her childhood ground, the limitless space granted to a prince. The world belonged to her, she was told, and all she surveyed was her birthright. These lands and these people, body and soul. Even the ruins of the defeated were hers to own. The al-Kattan, descended from the sun.

Now the land is unrecognizable to her ancestors, and those who stood with her as she beheaded Ihsayn are gone.

She swings down from the carriage and stands at the crematorium's gate. Looking for footprints will prove fruitless. The desert retains its nature and, even beneath snow, sand shifts like water. Instead she circles the area and waits for her senses to find their level. The scent is the thing that, to her, has changed the most about her homeland: there is dampness, there are low sedges that never grew in the desert and lichen that clings to ruins once coated only in dust, and they have laced the air with the smell of scrabbling life. Earthy, faintly green. In a few decades more, maybe this land will grow truly other, entirely removed from its desert past. Birds other than vultures and desert hummingbirds would perch on wrecked architecture and preen and build nests. The edges would run green and soft with dew, and at last the vision that inspired the al-Kattan founders—that infinity of sunlit gold—would dissolve.

Lussadh glances backward at the behemoth, the metropolis, that looms and cuts against the horizon. A city far more elevated, more resplendent, than Ihsayn's wildest ambitions and made in a shape the king would never have comprehended or accepted. Even from here, its cadences are visible—the carriages along the bridges, the trains arriving and departing, the rhythms of more than two hundred thousand lives.

She shields her face from the sun-glare. There is a possibility that her particular talent will fail; it has always worked best when another glass-bearer is near, a room or two away. But she has no other compass. Another possibility still is that she has ridden out like this for nothing, that her chase is as needless as the queen insisted, and she will find her lieutenant standing over the Heron, effortless and victorious. Or the pull between them will contract and they will draw toward one another, meeting at the precise midpoint between crematorium and city: Nuawa carrying the Heron's heart in a box and marching toward Kemiraj, then laughing bemused when she sees Lussadh. *Why are you here, General? I was just on the way, but what a delightful surprise. Let me take your arm.*

These are all possibilities. Some are more remote than others.

She strides in ever-widening circles. She can estimate neither distance nor direction, nor even when or if her senses will stir and rouse to Nuawa's presence. But she does not permit herself to panic.

When Lussadh does feel the tug, it is as fierce and jagged as thirst. She breaks into a run. The wasteland blurs, seams of silver light and charred stone, a sky as flat as paper and which presses down like a war-weight of dead.

Eventually she slows down, her breath knocking in her chest. This is how she finds her lieutenant:

A tableau in black and gray and white, untidily limned in blood. An impossible quantity, as if an abattoir has burst open here and drenched the earth. Lussadh feels nothing and then she does. Her throat closes as she draws near and kneels next to Nuawa. One hand pulped and shattered, the other loosely gripping her blade. She has fallen next to the Heron, whose chest lies bared to the sky, a cavity in which bloodless muscles and ice glitter. There isn't much of his head left.

Lussadh has imagined killing Nuawa before. She has pictured it clearly. Yet this is not the same, and when she bends to scoop Nuawa into her arms the lieutenant is unthinkably light, as though every drop of fluid has been vented from her and left her a hollow husk. "Nuawa," she whispers. The catch in her voice, fragile as old vows. It has been a long time since she has ever heard herself like this. The girl from Shuriam, and later —but there is a pulse; her lieutenant's heart still beats. She presses her finger to Nuawa's throat. Yes. The vital rhythm, faint yet extant. She looks her lieutenant over: the hemorrhage must have slowed down from the cold and Nuawa's heart must have been sustained by the queen's mirror. The sliver of power which will not allow its bearer to so easily fade.

She binds Nuawa's arm, above the ruin of wrist and hand, and wipes the vomit from the lieutenant's face. Nuawa's eyelids twitch. They open and Nuawa looks up at her, eyes glazed with pain. Then, "General?" Hoarse and broken, an echo of an echo.

"I'm here. You will be fine. You're fine. You're too strong to perish here."

Something like a grimace, like a smile. "I don't want you to see me like this. I must be dying. It's odd, I don't feel much of anything. Can you do me a favor?"

Lussadh traces the line of Nuawa's jaw with her fingertips. "I'll bring down the moon and drape every living star on your shoulders, and tie asteroids around your ankles. I'll put upon you more treasury than the sun itself owns."

The lieutenant tries to laugh. "The Heron's heart. The queen commanded me to bring it back."

It rests in the Heron's lap, a lump that resembles unrefined iron more than it does any organ. Lussadh takes it in hand, and even through her glove, it radiates a piercing chill. She slips it into her belt satchel. "I have it." She gathers Nuawa in her arms and touches her mouth to the lieutenant's brow. "We're going home."

TWELVE

THE GENERAL WAS right in that Nuawa was not dying. The palace chiurgeon gives her a transfusion—the source of it she cannot guess, though she assumes the donor is either well compensated or dead— and in a week she is back on her feet, though she does not like to look at the stump where her right hand used to be. Her operation included amputating what was left of it: the remaining bones and tissue were useless, on the path to necrosis.

At all times she covers herself in a heavy coat; she imagines she must look like a particularly bulky specter, wandering the palace at night. The dead of night, since she doesn't sleep much, and the servants avert their gazes when she passes. Major Guryin tries to ambush her, but she successfully avoids xer. Not to be deterred, xe knocks on her door morning and evening, and in the end slides short missives under her door. Reports of the state of things, gossip items. The general comes to see her once, and Nuawa turns Lussadh away too.

She thinks of the stories of animals that know their time and flee to a place where they may die in solitude. It is not accurate, but she understands the sentiment that went into this myth.

Major Guryin's little letters turn into a pile. She stops reading after the third or so. What Nuawa does is eat, to keep her body strong, and in idle times she would verify the sharpness of her sword, the readiness of her gun. Chamber fully loaded, trigger perfectly oiled. She becomes fascinated by the way light interacts with metal. In the short hours that she sleeps, that permeates her dreams. The material of guns, the material of bullets, and the illumination of lanterns or moon on both from this or that angle. This occupies her sleep more than even the Winter Queen.

It is peculiar to move with half an arm gone—her balance is not what she is used to, a missing limb and a missing weight. But she does what she can to stay limber, pacing her sickroom and then the hallways of the palace wing. She is wary, at first, that Lussadh will try to do what Guryin did and lie in wait in hidden alcoves. The general does not. For this, Nuawa is thankful. She knows herself, the tensility of her wit and heart, and she knows Lussadh would disturb her equilibrium. Nuawa does not allow herself to ponder such things as last wishes, what is left behind, what is left incomplete; nor does she allow herself to contemplate what she stands to lose. It was always mirage, the things she has gathered to her after she executed her mother.

The Heron's heart rests in a box at her bedside, enclosed in velvet and steel. Even through that she can see its light, palpitating like a heart under stress, a heart speeding toward annihilation. She muses on whether it contains his ghost too: *The fabric of existence is stitched by souls.*

Eventually the queen calls for her.

She meets the queen in what used to be the king's hall, with its high dais and its throne on which she and Lussadh fucked. The Winter Queen does not sit on that throne: instead she stands at the base. Despite the scale of this—the steep wide steps, the high petaled ceiling—she is not diminished; rather she seems greater than the mundane furniture, the mundane trappings of a mortal king and a dead dynasty. She's in full regalia, almost the same dress, Nuawa is certain, that she wore on the night Nuawa went into the kiln. The iron coronet, the armored robe, the crystals in her hair that forms out of her breath. The only piece not present is that wide blade that, Nuawa now knows, is more decorative than anything. The Winter Queen needs no weapons.

She kneels before the queen, presents the box with her one good hand. "The Heron's heart, as you have required."

Wordless, the queen takes it from her. The lid is lifted, and the velvet lining is discarded. She holds the heart, cradling it in her palm; contact with her skin makes it brighter still, gushing incandescence in lieu of blood that must have pumped through it many lifetimes ago. "Look at this," the queen murmurs, "the heart of my first retainer. More gorgeous than it ever was in flesh. I found him by a river, spearing fish, a child who knew nothing and who'd never seen the world beyond those banks. How we've all changed." The queen puts the heart into the folds of her robes. "In those days I would eat this to regain what he stole from me, but that's no longer necessary."

She nudges the iron box on the floor aside with her foot. Then she holds out her hand. "Now," the queen says, "your reward."

When the queen grips Nuawa, she strangles back every instinct to struggle free from a predator's grasp. White fingertips run across her brow, her cheeks, every point of contact like the tip of a frigid knife.

Against the mosaic wall the queen kisses her, and her vision shifts. The world sheds its lining, its surface, revealing what burns beneath. Between Nuawa and the royal mouth, a phantom umbilicus stretches, hairline-thin and translucent. A song begins in her heart, drums and cicadas and bells, and her mouth overflows with sweetness. This time, painfully, there is arousal. To lie bare and ajar before the queen; in her this imperative rears and buckles like a rutting gold-eyed thing. The queen's skin is warm and pliant.

She does not lose herself. She had the presence of mind to act while the Heron took hold of her; she has the presence of mind now. The queen's armor is ornamental, and there are openings in the front. She shoves the muzzle of her gun against the queen's breast, saying nothing, offering neither threats nor declarations. With her legs she clings to the queen, and with her hand she pulls the trigger.

Had the queen been anyone else there would be guards in this room and she'd have instantly been riddled with bullets, but the Winter Queen has never seen the need for human soldiers to defend her.

The queen crumples. There is blood, a vast amount, pooling under her and spreading out wider than her robes. Nuawa keeps firing: fore-head, throat, heart again.

A force lifts her off her feet and flings her into the wall. She tries to get a fourth shot off as ice grows over her limbs, in webs and inele-gant chains, pinning her in place. Nuawa strains against them, yanking and kicking. She may as well strain against a mountain; she subsides. No point wasting her strength, even now; there may still be an opening—an opportunity—anything.

The queen comes to her knees and clutches at the rupture in her chest. Her mouth is red, and she bares her teeth at Nuawa. "How quaint," she hisses, "that the Heron thought my old weakness remains. He must've told you? Nor was he wrong, precisely."

Where her heart or some analogous organ resides, the wound fills and closes. In less than a minute her flesh is paper-smooth, nearly as white. "He underestimated, my old servant, how much I have grown since his parting with me. And you have overestimated the strength of your mortality. You were able to make me bleed; you were able to turn me nearly human, for just a moment ... but you've changed too much inside, Lieutenant, your mortal essence has been diluted. My mirror transmutes its hosts, and you've been bearing it—activated—your entire life. And so, you could not contaminate me with vulnerable flesh, vulnerable blood. You never could have."

Nuawa's breathing comes fast and her tongue seems suddenly too large for her mouth, but she does not let her gun go.

"How long have you been plotting this, I wonder? All your life? When Lussadh came across you, ah, what a stroke of luck that must have been." The queen runs her hand down the lines of her robes, dismissing the blood. Red dollops fall to the floor, seeping into tiles, into the cracks between stone. The silk and armor return to immacu-lacy. "These months you must have watched for any weakness, clawed at every secret you can get your hand on, dreamed up a hundred scenarios and more. Along came the Heron. I'm surprised the two of you didn't negotiate, but then *he* was never the sort to work with anybody. No. It was always him, himself alone that must deliver the blow. And you, how did you picture this? Did you hope I would gaze into your eyes and see my demise, did you hope I would beg for my life? Were you anticipating being hailed as a hero, the one who changes it all and brings peace to these lands? Perhaps venerated as a living saint."

"I am not," Nuawa says softly, "afraid to die."

The queen laughs, a little wetly. "I suppose you are not."

One strand of frost snakes around Nuawa's neck—she tenses—and pushes its way into her mouth. It is tender, at first, probing the way a lover's finger might. It wraps around her tongue, rubs against her teeth. Then it pours down her throat. She gags around the ice—her gun drops from slack fingers—as it sleets into her stomach, hooking into her intestines, her spine. Something is wrenched out and she briefly tastes the sourness of it, the slippery texture of insect shell.

She coughs up blood as the parasite writhes before her eyes, glistening and suspended aloft. It has grown immense inside her, segmented and studded with more legs and cilia than she can count, its head helmed in nacreous carapace. Cobalt mandibles twitch uselessly as it thrashes against the grip of the queen.

Whose smile grows wide, at Nuawa, at the creature. "So, you poisoned yourself. Was this meant for my general? Who can say. Certainly, it would not have worked against me. Either way, you won't be needing this." The queen clenches her fist.

The parasite's shriek is strangely human, even though it could not possibly have the necessary vocal cords; it sounds, Nuawa realizes, mostly like her. It splatters on the tiles, heavy with her fluids. Lymph and saliva and stomach acids.

Her thoughts are blank. There is no more last resort. "Kill me, then."

The Winter Queen's head tilts, so far sideways that her neck cannot possibly support it. "Such a duty is beneath me. It falls to Lussadh to undertake it, the execution of a treasonous glass-bearer. That is the entire purpose for which I chose her. To lead, and to punish when it is required: my general, my sword. Do you have a preference, Nuawa? A bullet, a blade, or some other more esoteric means? There is starvation, there is drowning, there is quartering. I may even give special dispensation for a bonfire, for I understand it is the

Sirapirat way to be cremated. Whatever the method you select, Lussadh will be the one to carry it out."

Nuawa says nothing. She will die, one way or another. That has always been a conclusion foregone, a conclusion she's accepted since she was eight. Even if she'd succeeded it would have been the same.

"Lussadh will do it," the queen goes on. "On my command, and because your crime is so great. Unforgivable both to me and to her. Yet being alive or dead is all the same to you." The queen puts a long, near-colorless finger to her own lips. "The real punishment is in my general's pain. Is that not so? The cold terror she will feel, watching you sink into the tides or standing there as you cook atop a pyre. The anguish that will grip her as she puts that bullet in your skull. Tell me, Nuawa, do you feel nothing for her after all? She has loved you so well, given you so much, honored you in every regard. Her passion runs deep, and it will wound her to put you down. For a long time, this grief will lodge in her like a knife. Is that all right, Nuawa? Can you bear leaving that behind, leaving her behind in such a condition?"

Nuawa continues her silence. She turns her face away; she closes her eyes. But the queen lowers her and a hand cups her chin, forcing her forward. One thumb dips into her mouth and it is so frigid that she cries out.

"I think," the queen says, "I already have my answer. But I want to hear it from you, aloud. Will it be so terrible, to stay alive, and to serve? I will keep Lussadh ignorant of your perfidy, and so will you. This way she can be spared all that trouble."

"Kill me," Nuawa rasps.

"Why would I?" The queen holds her head immobile. She is close enough to kiss Nuawa again. "Let it not be said that I have in myself no mercy. You shall strike where I point, act as I require. Not so different from what you've been doing. And my general you can still have, and you shall delight each other gloriously. So, what will it be, Nuawa?"

———

AS A CHILD LUSSADH loved the desert sunset, the totality of it, the clear unobstructed line that consumes the horizon. A pure tableaux, an unblemished geometry. She stands on the balcony, tasting the wind and the conjunction of fire and sky that has made a red canvas of her city. Kemiraj has returned to its normal self, busy and loud with passage of trains. Incoming ones loaded with officials to replace casualties lost to the coup, outgoing ones loaded with stranded visitors and occidentals desperate to return home. The evening markets are opening, lanterns coming on like night-blooming roses. Strains of percussive music drift skyward, accompanied by kites advertising the wares and services of moneyed artisans. Pennants fly high, bearing the queen's insignia and face, her image reflected a hundred times over. Some more refined, some less so—there are portraits of her engraved on roofs that are almost garish in their competition to outdo others in vividity, bright and exaggerated.

She doesn't greet Nuawa until her lieutenant is next to her, a silhouette made heavy with a dark flared coat. Nuawa holds her arms close to her, the amputated one hidden inside a long oxblood sleeve. "Are you displeased with me, General?"

"No. What for?" Still Lussadh does not reach out: something tells her Nuawa will not wish to be touched yet.

"That I didn't want to be seen and very rudely sent you away when you tried to visit." Nuawa's face is half-veiled by shadow, in profile. "I'm a fighter first and foremost. A duelist—or soldier—with one hand is a pathetic sight."

"There's more to you than your prowess in combat."

"Is there?" The lieutenant's smile is empty. "It has been my life. I am—I was—rather good at it, if I may be so arrogant. I'm not sure where else I could apply myself. I know a thing or two about horticulture but have never developed a talent. I am literate, but so are most people. I'm useless at any craft or trade. At best I might be a critic of the arts, and we know how useful those are."

"You could be anything you want, Nuawa," Lussadh says gently. "To raise fierce animals, to make fine things. Or to continue as you are —one hand less will not unmake you, and I have at my command the best chiurgeons in winter. They can make for you a new limb, a perfect prosthesis. Whatever it takes, if you want it, you will have it."

Nuawa touches her right shoulder. Her hand pulls away before it reaches the point where the elbow ends. "And I'm ambidextrous. Yet even that will take time, I understand; my body may reject the prosthesis. Anything could happen and while I try to make myself whole again—as whole as what's left of this can be—I will be of no use to you."

"Wrong." Lussadh does draw the lieutenant to her now, lightly, letting Nuawa know she can pull aside when she wishes. "You are more than your utility. You're far more important than what you can do with a gun."

A short, abortive laugh. "Am I? To what am I so important?"

"To—" Lussadh takes a breath. She remembers sharply the sensation of discovering her lieutenant in the snow. That moment, that frisson. "To me. You're important to me, more than I can possibly say. Nuawa, marry me."

The lieutenant stiffens, turning to face Lussadh. "General?"

"I'm asking for your hand. To be my wife." She could say, *You make my blood sing, as few others have*. But it seems a poor confession when those others, save the queen, are bone and dust. "It's sudden, I realize, and too soon. And this is not a question I've thought of putting before you until now, because I haven't thought in these terms for decades. Yet I want to ask it, because I know that if I didn't, I would curse myself for a coward for the rest of my days. Were you to say no, it will still have been worth the asking, for I'd have proven my courage."

Nuawa stares at her, mouth opening then closing. When she laughs again, it sounds much less like the beginning of weeping. "I don't know what to say. I would never expect this of you. In fact, I never expected anyone to ... ask for my hand."

"Take your time," Lussadh says quickly. "No matter your decision, I vow that you will have a place at my side, a place of honor and freedom to do and be as you please."

"I don't think I will take any sort of time. My entire life I've always made my choices the way I draw my gun. Without hesitation. This is not where I thought I would be, and you're important to me. Inasmuch as I can say such a thing, and maybe that is how the heart makes its own exegesis. There is a barrier in all of us between the apparatus that thinks and the apparatus that feels." Nuawa shakes her head, blinking as if she is waking from a dream. "Please ask me again, General."

Lussadh is smiling when she says, "Nuawa Dasaret, my lieutenant, will you be my bride?"

"Yes." Nuawa reaches for her, stretching on tiptoes to meet Lussadh. "I accept. Yes, General Lussadh al-Kattan, commander of winter, I will be your bride."

ABOUT THE AUTHOR

Benjanun Sriduangkaew writes love letters to strange cities, beautiful bugs, and the future. Her work has appeared on Tor.com, in *Beneath Ceaseless Skies*, *Clarkesworld*, and year's best collections. She was short-listed for the Campbell Award for Best New Writer, and her debut novella *Scale-Bright* was nominated for the British SF Association Award. She is the author of *Winterglass, Mirrorstrike*, and *And Shall Machines Surrender*. She has lived in Bangkok, Hong Kong, and Jakarta.

For more information:
https://beekian.wordpress.com/

ALSO BY BENJANUN SRIDUANGKAEW

Winterglass

Made in the USA
Coppell, TX
22 December 2020

46948229R10083